The Curse of Dawn

Coda Languez

Published by Coda Languez, 2022.

THE CURSE OF DAWN

First edition. May 11, 2022.

ISBN: 979-8201303884

Written by Coda Languez.

Table of Contents

Note From the Author

This is a standalone novella that is a modern and gender bent take on 'Beauty and the Beast'. As the setting is contemporary, there is a lot of modern language and the POV is that of a veteran suffering from PTSD and anxiety. Due to the dark nature of this 'aged-up' tale, below is a list of content warnings:

- Coarse language: Intermittent strong language throughout the story

- Sex / Nudity: Mild sexual content and nudity in the following chapters

  ◦ 'One Night' has the beginning of a sexual encounter

  ◦ 'A Lonely Morning' has a reference to a sexual act

  ◦ 'Nighttime Affairs' has mild but crude descriptions

  ◦ 'A Happy Dream' has the start of a sexual encounter

- Violence: The MC is a veteran and has scarring throughout his body. The following chapters have graphic descriptions of gore and violence:

  ◦ 'A Nightmare Awakening' details a horrific hallucination

  ◦ 'The Witch's Curse' discusses genocide and destruction of a nation

∘ 'The Dawn's Kiss' details horrific imagery

• Other: Both main characters suffer from depression and thus have suicidal ideation. Remorse, guilt, and anxiety are large part of the narrative. If you or someone you know is going through a hard time and expressing thoughts of self-harm, please consider reaching out to this number below:

∘ **National Suicide Prevention Hotline**

▪ **1-800-273-TALK (8255)**

Chapter One
A Curse

In the darkness of night, the moon is the only light.
Your beauty will be as fair as your heart.
But in the brightness of day, the sun enters the fray.
You will be a nightmare, destined to be torn apart.

Chapter Two
Icarus And The Moon

"The view is wonderful, isn't it?"

My fists tightened around the iron railing. Just when I was ready for the long dive, the abrupt voice snapped my survival instincts into action.

I closed my eyes, swallowing mucus and bile back down into my stomach. I looked up from the ground 30 floors below and towards the deep purple and pink-colored mountains that peeked between the skyscrapers of downtown.

It was a radiant view.

I sighed, looking to the side.

I didn't come here to admire the sights and sounds of the city, nor the majestic views of the western peaks.

There is solely one reason a man would hang off the rooftop of a hotel, 30 stories above the asphalt below.

"You should go back inside." My voice was an indistinct murmur as I took a tiny step forward from the narrow ledge. My shoulder blades pushed against the jagged edges of the brick, my back arching as I willed my toes forward, my instincts forcing my upper back to sink as far as it could to the wall.

"So you can hog this glorious sight to all of yourself?"

I clenched my teeth, sweat rolling down my forehead and stinging my eyes, forcing my lids to clench close. That voice was teasing, yet gentle. A playful soprano that danced along my ears. I should just push myself upwards, letting momentum tumble me parallel to the ground below, letting me fall and fall and fall until the inevitable splatter.

However, no longer did instinct prevent me from doing just that.

Now it was curiosity.

I opened my eyes, releasing a huff through my nose as I looked over my shoulder to the interruptor of my suicide, "Why the hell does it matter to-"

I think I have seen this scene play out before.

Not with some loser who is looking for a very permanent exit. However, I have watched this before. Zoning out in front of the TV, left on Lifetime, something like that.

A young man, flawless face, even more flawless body, some kind of bad boy locks eyes with the most beautiful woman he's even seen and it's...

It's love at first sight.

God, it hurts.

Why did it have to be ME she looked at?

Fuck, why did I have to stare at her? Why now?!

Didn't I decide to just go 'fuck it' to everything?

Why, when everything was so god damn empty, when the idea of living one more god awful day was EXHAUSTING... did I have to see her?

When she tilted her head, her eyebrows arching upwards while her eyes twinkled with the stars in the arriving night sky. Her lips parted as I realized that was staring at her with my mouth slack-jawed.

Which was perfect?

Of course, her one and only memory of my dumbass would've been of me gawking at her before becoming a tiny red splatter on the ground far below. Like a terrible yet super expensive painting in a modern art museum we would visit-

Oh, good.

I'm already imagining us on dates.

Fan-fucking-tastic.

I tore my traitorous eyes away from her. As much as I hoped looking to the ground would focus me back on my goal, those sparkling, dark eyes drilled into the back of my head. I closed my eyes, my teeth ground together as her hair and their silky tendrils danced along my ear. Was she leaning over the railing to get closer to me?

Her voice still held that enchanting melody. "I'm wondering if the view is better from where you are. I thought that being on the rooftop is enough." The song of her giggle was like tiny bells dancing along the breeze. "But maybe I need a more exhilarating peek."

I balked, "You don't need to do that! Just go back inside, okay?!"

"Why? I think enjoying the evening is better with company, right?"

Fuck! Is she dense, or stubborn?! Isn't it obvious what I'm going to do?! "I don't want company and trust me, you don't want mine."

"I don't think so."

"I am very shitty company. Go back inside." I tilted my head up again, faking a brave smirk, "There is an outstanding lounge just one floor below. They made me an exceptional Manhattan. With a limited release of bourbon. You should try it."

"I should, then I'd be brave daredevil like you." Her eyes glittered as her lips curled into a genuine smile.

It hurt so much, "Just... just fuck off all right?! I'm not here for the view and I don't want you to watch this! Go back inside!" I blinked, my eyes getting misty and vision fogging up. "Enjoy your night. Don't let me ruin it."

Her form was fuzzy, and she was the most enchanting Gaussian blur. I watched those foggy shoulders sag, accompanied by a soft sigh, and finally, after seconds that felt like years, that form moved away from the edge.

My heart stopped when she disappeared from view. When I looked forward to the blues and purples of the night sky, my hands sunk from the railing and to my sides.

I didn't want it to end this way.

With regret instead of relief.

Oh well.

What's not one more bit of misery for a sendoff?

"Dang it! My favorite shoe!"

My eyes widened as I saw a peach high-heeled shoe zoom past my head. I knew it was peach because, much like my life flashing before my eyes, it was falling in slow motion before vanishing into the trafficked light abyss below. I turned my head to the side, my mouth gulping in air like a panicked fish out of water as the woman from before lowered herself over the railing. Without a second thought, I jerked my shoulder over to grab onto butt, trying to force her back over the edge, "WHAT THE FUCK ARE YOU DOING?"

Her legs playfully kicked the railing, her hands holding onto the bars, the only thing keeping her from death. "What? I wanted to join you!"

Is this beautiful idiot drunk?! "Are you out of your mind?!" I heaved as I shoved her back over the rail, not caring about the squeaking 'OOF' she released when she hit the roof. I gasped, my upper body almost flailing back before my core muscles, driven by my rebellious survival instincts, clenched and I grabbed onto the bars again. Sweat cascaded down my cheeks like a waterfall, and I looked up at her face.

She was trying to go over the god damn rail again!

"Are you crazy?!" I grit my teeth and pull myself up, nearly head-butting her away. "Why are you doing this?!"

Her laugh was the most melodic yet annoying song to my ears. "I thought you might want company."

"No! I don't want company!" My eyes watered again and my voice swelled against the night breeze. "I WANT TO DIE!"

"Why?"

I blinked, a tear joining the sweat dripping down my chin.

Her smile left, and her lips pressed together. Her black hair moved liked waves over the breeze and her eyes, still sparkling with the stars, studied me.

Why...?

Cause it hurts.

Cause living hurts.

Cause being unable to sleep hurts.

Cause going through the motions day after day takes so much out of me, then I fall on the floor in my shitty apartment in pain.

Cause my friends can barely stand me.

Cause the other half of my friends are already dead and fuck, I am so goddamn jealous of them!

Cause I'm numb.

So numb and so heavy.

I am a rusted anchor sinking in quicksand and I am so... so tired.

Let me fall-

I shudder, feeling feathery touches on my cheek, just next to my eye, where another tear fell. Delicate fingers in my periphery wiped away the moisture, and I was dumbstruck.

She smiled again and lowered her chest over the railing. Thick locks of velvet brushed against my face as her lips crept closer, her breath against my ear. "I'm going to keep climbing over until you come up here instead."

Why do you care?

That question climbed up my throat.

Why do you care?

I can feel words clamoring to escape.

Why do you care?!

Yet when she lifted herself up and hoisted herself over, that question died and I pulled myself up first, gripping her shoulders and pushing her away.

She gripped my shirt and as she fell back; the momentum hauled me over.

On top of her.

My hands landed besides her shoulders and I pushed myself up, panting as adrenaline rocked through me.

I was lying on top of the most beautiful woman in world and while I silenced for the 50th time in the past few minutes; she was laughing.

Was she laughing at the absurdity of this moment? Or was she laughing because she's alive... and I'm alive... and that gave her joy?

What... what the hell?

She covered her mouth, trying to stifle giggles. "Wow! That was so close, huh?! We almost died!" Her shoulders shook, the strap of her ivory and peach dress slipping off her shoulders, "Oh my god!" She slowly slid back, sitting up and cupping my blank stupid face in her delicate hands, "Are you okay?"

Am I... am I okay?

My shoulders sagged and all of my muscles came loose.

I... I wanted to die.

I was so close. Close to finally ending my misery.

Yet, relief.

I survived the night.

I looked into those starry eyes and a chuckle escape my lips. A chuckle that grew into a laugh. "You... you're a crazy bitch, you know that?"

Her lips puckered, and her cheeks puffed up as if she was a toddler. However, no offense showed in her glittering eyes, "Rude! You should never call a lady that!" She kept the air hoarded in her cheeks as her sigh released it. Her hands let go of my cheeks. "I'm glad that you're alive."

"Yeah, me too."

I have been hearing this one word repeat in my head and with more disbelief than the last.

What?

WHAT?

I was... happy to be alive. Not even a minute after I was just an inch a way from ending it all.

This woman, this smiling stranger... saved my life.

Chapter Three
Salud to Life

"You were right."

"About what?"

"This Manhattan is AH-MAZING."

The gorgeous hero across from me set down her empty glass, a pink blush across her apple cheeks.

I looked down towards my cognac loaded drink. "Honestly, I didn't even know. I overheard a real fancy couple talk about them." Lifting the glass, I took a short gulp. "They don't skimp on the good stuff, at least. That burns nicely."

She rested her elbows on the table, the side of her head relaxed on the back of her hands. "I should try that one next. What'd you get? A sidecar?"

My shoulders shook slightly, trying to keep in a laugh. "Haven't you had enough?"

"I still have the jitters! We almost died!" Her head straightened, her eyes going wide with another gasp, "Oh my god, we almost died! That would wake anyone up!"

My chuckle turned into a bit of a guffaw. "My adrenaline was going nuts. I mean, I was ready. I was so ready. Then a freaking crazy lady tries climbing over." My eyes narrowed as I pointed accusingly at her, "A suicidal sap does not want a beautiful woman's death on their conscious."

Those plump lips widened and her eyes lidded, lashes fluttering, "Such a burden to place on your soul. You would've been haunting this hotel, missing all of this liquor."

Thank god she let my desperate compliment pass. I wonder if the alcohol was hitting me harder due to surviving my suicide attempt. I stared at the golden mixture in my glass, a question dancing along the tip of my tongue. "Why were you on the roof?"

She shrugged, looking away from me to the bar. The heat lamp shone orange and yellow along her face. "You don't believe I was there for the view?"

"No. I thought you were just drunk, but that definitely didn't turn out to be the case."

Her smile stayed on her face, but the stars that twinkled in her eyes faded. "Maybe I saw you and thought 'Oh, that sounds like a good idea.'"

The center of my brow knotted tightly. "Why the hell did you think that?!" My voice came out in a sudden growl and I regretted instantly.

Who the fuck was I to judge?

Though, the idea of her falling, of that light suddenly going out, pissed me off.

It terrified me.

Her eyes closed, and she laughed, though it didn't hold the same joy. "I'm going to let that slide. Considering you told me to fuck off and let you die."

I flinched as she cursed for the first time this night, placing my palm over my big mouth. I sighed, shoulders sagging in shame as I lowered my hand. "You're right. Still, you dying with a loser like me? I'd hate myself more than I already do."

"How would I feel if I stood by and did nothing?" Her smile was gone, and she studied me again with those dark eyes. Eyes as ancient as the rings of a fossilized tree.

My brow furrowed again, and heat ran up my neck. "You'd feel like shit." I gripped the stem of my glass tightly, teeth clenched. "So was it an obli-obligation or something?"

Her eyes softened, and she shook her head. "You make it sound like you are a burden and you are not." She tilted her head, and those lips parted, her brow lifting, "You needed some company... and so did I. Could we be kindred spirits? Either way, while I'm here, I don't want you to think so little of yourself."

I snorted, though she released all the air from my indignation. "You can't control that."

I can't control that.

She giggled again, the sound soft. "True, I can't. However, people would be sad if you'd died."

My eyes narrowed and, I took another gulp, the cognac burning down into my stomach before I set the glass down, "You don't know that. You don't know what I have put people through."

"Okay, fine." She moved her drink to the side and leaned closer towards me. "I would be sad if you died."

"You barely know me."

"Yet I care enough to save your life, right?"

She did, but only a monster would stand by and do nothing.

Humans must save each other—

I stopped myself from saying it.

Was there someone else who would climb over the railing to join me?

Someone else who would risk certain death for a stranger and be freaking stubborn for some stranger?

My eyes shifted forwards to her, taking in the glow of the heat lamp along her apple cheeks, the orange hue dancing over those lips. Her dark eyes reminded me of the nebulas in space, as ancient and as beautiful as the rings on a tree.

She cared enough to save my life and enough to remind me of the thrill of living.

My lips parted, but I was too dumbstruck to say anything, to argue back. My fingers curled along the glass table, nails attempting to scratch the frosted surface.

However, before I can try to incur damages from the bar, her hand gently pressed against the back of mine, delicate digits softly stroking the coarse skin over my bones and veins.

I was so unworthy. I was the plague and if she kept touching me like that, she would catch the void and be swallowed whole.

However, I didn't want her to stop.

Her touch, her presence...

My heart was pounding so hard it reminded me how ALIVE I was.

She tilted her head, her eyes lidded and her voice a whisper. "Would you like to join me for the night?"

She barely knows me.

Yet she cared enough to want to take a leap into the end with me. So I wouldn't be alone...

"Yeah. I do."

Chapter Four
I Think I Think Too Much

What was I doing?

"This is it."

My heart is bursting inside of my ribs.

She inserted the keycard.

I jumped like a kid when the lock clicked open.

Her small hand gently wrapped around mine.

Delicate.

Frail.

My hand was so much bigger than hers.

I could crush her.

So... why was I here?

I know my palms were coated with sweat, yet she still pulled forward.

What the fuck was I doing?!

I stood inside of a strange woman's room.

My heart pounded loudly in my chest.

She was talking to me.

The words distorted.

My ears filled with fluid.

Why was I here?

She invited me.

I am a stranger to her.

A strange man who tried to throw himself off of a random hotel building.

Why did she invite me?

Was it really because she liked my company?

My mind felt heavy.

There was an anchor hooked into it, dragging it down into a familiar void.

There was no way she liked me.

Not enough to bring me into her room.

A small, beautiful woman like her brought an unstable, suicidal stranger into her fancy hotel room.

I didn't deserve to be here.

I'm scum.

Why did she bring me here?

No way did she like my company.

The void...

It's weighing me down, devouring any happiness I had ignorantly enjoyed.

We barely talked long enough for her to be attracted to me.

She was so beautiful; there so many people better for her.

So why me?

Because... she pitied me?

"Hey... are... okay...?"

She asked something. I heard it. She asked me something and I don't know what to say!

The door shut behind us.

She was locked in with me.

An unstable, sorry piece of shit.

... That's it.

It was a pity.

She didn't like me.

No one liked me.

She pitied me.

My brow narrowed sharply into a throbbing knot.

I was so stupid.

Why else would she invite me into her room?!

She pitied me.

She didn't see me as attractive.

She didn't see me as a man.

"St-stop..."

That was my voice.

I didn't want to say that out loud. It was supposed to be to the void! The fog was so heavy.

How could I possibly think she actually wanted to be with me?

Soft, small finger tips touched my cheeks, and I almost jumped.

Was she always so close?!

Why was she touching me?

"... Ome... ack..."

What was she saying?

Her touch trailed against my face, and my cheeks burned. Blood pulsed from my hammering heart down to my dick, and I hated myself even more.

"... ey... ome... ba..."

My hands reached up to grip her wrists.

Her thin wrists. Skin soft like silk. That she would want me for a one-night stand was ridiculous. I was desperate. Desperate enough to say yes to someone who couldn't see me as a man.

I'm not a man.

I'm a piece of shit.

I'm a suicidal piece of shit and she pitied me.

My hands trembled, and my grip around her frail wrists tightened.

I didn't want her to be sorry for me.

Fuckin' Christ, that's why I'm here!

She wanted to monitor me.

Make sure I don't go jumping off rooftops.

I had 60 pounds on her!

There was no fucking way she can even try to stop me!

So don't pity me!

Don't think that you I was a fucking stray dog you picked up!

God, even through this dark fog, her eyes twinkled like the stars in the sky. She didn't even flinch in my grip. If it wasn't for her expression, I could delude myself into thinking that she wanted me.

Her brow was arched up, her dark, ringed eyes wide and watery. Her lips, plump, pressed together, and she tilted her head and asked me the one question that confirmed all my fears.

My head was above water and I understood her.

"Are you all right?"

No. No, I was not all right.

I'm was the opposite side of the world from 'all right.'

She didn't see any anything but a piece of suicidal shit!

She had to watch over me!

I was a burden.

No one saw me as a man.

Just a burden.

My enormous hands released her wrists, and this time my palms were on her cheeks. I lowered my head, staring into the stars in her eyes and begging for the illusion to come back. That she invited me here because she wanted me.

That I MEAN something to her.

Her lips are so close, and the all-consuming void removes its tendrils from my brain a little so I can have a moment to think that this stranger sees me as anything but a piece of shit.

Anything but a load to carry.

Those lips parted, "Wait..."

I shattered.

The void tendrils go sharp and drill into my head, sucking away any serotonin, any good or peace into its abyssal gullet.

I was numb.

I was broken.

I was in pieces strewn across her hotel room floor and I was too fucked up to put myself together. "Why did you... invite me here?"

"Because I wanted to."

"That's not an answer." I knew the answer. It laughed at me and as soon as I left, she would too.

That or thankful that the mood lightened with my exit. "Why am I here? Is it because... just... just say it! Why?"

"I like you." A small smile danced along her lips and I'm mocked. "I wanted your company. Why do I need another reason?"

I clenched my teeth. I swore I heard a crack from how tightly my teeth ground together.

She lied.

"You invited a strange man into your room."

She nodded, and I kept my palms on her face, just so my ears don't fill up with mud, "And you accepted the invitation of a strange woman."

"You're small and I overpower you..."

"I bided my time on the drugs. I may have snuck into your drink."

Just tell me you pitied me.

I was a pitiful piece of shit and you felt sorry for me.

"I'm unstable. A mess."

"... I know."

My heart broke as she spoke the truth so painfully. Tears welled up and the fucking void is pulled me down into myself.

It would devour me like quicksand.

"I am too." Her hands touched the back of mine and her smile widened, one eyebrow raised slightly higher than the other. "I meant it, when I said I wanted to join you."

What the hell?

This beautiful woman had so much more to lose and so much more to live for.

Why would she want to end it?

The goddamn void was hissing into my ears. Burning acid steam poked holes into my eardrums.

Lies...

Her fingers intertwined with mine, and she leaned closer. Now I'm the one leaning back, the shadows impaled on my thoughts. "Wait..."

She did.

I outweighed her, and I was stronger than her.

If I wanted to fuck her, there was nothing she could do to stop me.

If I wanted to walk out and throw myself off the nearest ledge, she couldn't do jack shit.

So why... why was I so powerless?

I needed to stop the tears.

They made me so pathetic; such a piece of shit.

... Ome... ack... ey... ome... ba... Hey... come back...

So that's what she was saying.

I closed my eyes, the tears not stopping, "... My head's heavy."

I was too weak to fight it.

"Then sleep with me."

"You don't want me."

"... I meant sleep, but if you wanted sex, I'm not opposed." She leaned her head against one of my palms, like a kitten nuzzling for more strokes. "We survived the night."

I wished I hadn't.

But she would've fallen with me.

We were fucking disasters.

The void didn't let go. It's stubbornly latched on. Yet She doesn't let it pull me away.

She would not leave me alone even though I'm a burden.

"...everything's heavy..."

She stepped back once, then twice, but one hand still stayed tied together with mine. "Come on, lay down. We've been standing for a while."

I let her guide me to the bed, and I sat down. Too afraid to let go of her hand, I gripped it as tightly as I gripped her wrists earlier. My breaths coming out so hard my lungs tried to puncture themselves on my ribs.

She sat down next to me and pushed me back.

I collapsed.

I'm a piece of shit dirtying the luxurious hotel sheets.

She placed her head on my shoulder, and I remember how close we were to the rooftop.

The exhilaration of that moment felt nothing like this did.

Peaceful.

It's peaceful, and I don't deserve it.

"I'm... I'm sorry..." I placed my forearm over my eyes. I swear my tears should dry up, but my eyes were swollen from all the fluid, "I'm sorry... you deserve better. You deserve a good night. Not some sack of shit taking it all away."

She pressed the top of her head under my chin. "I don't see a sack of shit here."

God, I would've bursted out laughing at hearing such an elegant curse if I wasn't drowning.

"I am with a kindred spirit."

"... You are strange. You're crazy."

Her small fingers wiped away the salty streams down my cheeks. "So are you."

I couldn't argue with that. For once, she and I agreed.

We were in total sync.

Chapter Five
One Night

I don't know how long we laid there together.
Five minutes.
Ten.
An hour.
I didn't know.

At some point, my head stopped hurting, and the void released me from its grasp.

The sharp tendrils had feasted enough.

Pathetic.

I turned my head to look down at the strangest woman I have ever met. Not seeing her eyes and being under the cover of darkness, I assumed she was asleep.

I lifted my head and gently shifted to move away from her, only to gasp in surprise as her fingers on my chest curled. My shirt trapped in her grip, she looked up at me with her lips turned to the side and her cheeks puffed up like a child. "Where do you think you're going?"

"I thought you were asleep, so... I was going to head out-"

"Nope. Stay."

Well, shit.

I was fucking powerless. "Okay."

I lower my head back down to the bed and gaze up at the ceiling.

The night was still and the darkness, once an enemy, was oddly calming.

Which would be a good thing.

Except now, I could focus on her breath against my neck.

Fuck, that was distracting.

Her fingers loosened their grip and now were idly stroking my chest.

My cheeks were scorching, and instead of tears, I was sweating.

Am I thirteen again?!

Just hitting puberty and discovering the dark, accessible joys of the internet?!

For fuck's sake, I already think I'm a shitty scumbag. Could my body NOT be so weak?!

The void was coming back, seeking dessert.

"Hey, you all right?"

Why did she ask that again?

"I'm... I should go."

I said that, but I'm still laying down.

I don't want to move.

"Do you want to go?"

No.

I don't want to go.

I haven't felt this safe and comfortable ever since I got back.

I want to stay here with her.

I'm so scared of ruining it.

"Hey... did you disappear again?" She lifted her head and shifted upwards. Her fingers pressed against my cheek and with that simple touch, my head turned towards her. My eyes focused on hers and again we are so close.

I couldn't think. Everything was rushing down from her touch and into my groin, and I hated myself for it. "I... I'm ruining this. Being here... it's nice and I know I will ruin it. So..so I have to go."

"No, you don't. Besides, you're not ruining anything." Her eyes were lidded and her lips brushed against mine, sending another jolt of burning need for me. "I don't want you to feel that way."

"I-I can't help it."

I really can't. I've tried for too long to control it.

It was too much to bear and she wouldn't let me end it.

Her fingers moved a lock of my hair behind my ear and shivers of delight shuddered down my neck to my spine, before caressing the edge of my ear. I moaned, my eyes fluttering as silk brushed against my skin, my hand running against her side. I wanted to touch her skin, and let goosebumps travel with my fingertips.

"Let me help you..."

The inevitable happened.

I pressed my lips against hers and to my complete shock; she kissed back, her lips parting.

Everything clicked.

Everything made sense.

Or at least, with our lips pressed together, tongues and tastes mixing, I could pretend it did.

This went against my truth.

The demonic void was shouting the truth to me.

Yet her head tilted to the side and I rolled onto my back, pulling her on top of me, letting this illusion flourish.

Yes, I know it was real, but there was no way, okay?

No way she saw me as anything but a lost puppy to watch over.

Even if she was making out with that pathetic mutt.

My hands reached under her blouse and gripped her waist, fingers stroking her smooth, hot skin. She was sweating too.

She moaned into my mouth and my truth was cracking; thin, jagged lines cut through its stubborn but flimsy veneer.

Maybe...she wanted me...

When I pulled back, our lips were wet and swollen from the desperate kiss. I gripped her waist tightly, fingers trembling as they dug into her flesh, "If... if I stay and we go-go further..." Yup, I was a teenager again, red-faced with absolutely no fucking idea what I was doing, "Then uh... I don't have any... any..."

Her face was flushed, and she giggled softly, kissing my forehead, then my nose. Her lips left a gentle mark on each cheek and she paused just before she reached my lips. "Condoms?"

I wanted to hide my face under the covers. This was embarrassing, "Y-yeah..."

She giggled against and sat up, her hips against mine. When she leaned to the side, her lower body shifted, and I groaned, biting my bottom lip. I stared at the ceiling, hearing the creak of a drawer sliding open. She jerked her hips a little more in search and I gasped.

She must've been doing this on purpose.

Her face came into view, her ebony hair cascading down either side of my face, a canopy blocking everything from my sight. Everything but her alluring face and enchanting eyes. She pressed her forehead against mine and chuckled as she tapped a packet against my cheek. "There. One less thing to stress over."

I was ashamed that conflicting emotions came over me. Relief and then irritation. My eyes narrowed and she must've noticed my look because her lips puckered together and she tilted her head, meeting my glare with one of her own.

Silently we judged each other, before I huffed and broke first, "Were... were you planning on a one-night stand? Did... did it matter who?"

She sat up again; the ceiling seemed so much closer than before. "Sometimes I wonder what people are thinking. Then the question is so obvious." She frowned, eyes burrowing into mine, the stars and rings gazing underneath my skin, "The answer is obvious too..."

I fucked it up and needed to take it back. "I mean..."

How do I fix this?

I can't fix it.

I fucked it up. I did, I ruined it.

My heart was squeezed so tightly it felt like it could burst and I was losing control of my breaths, "I'm sorry, I didn't- I just..."

Her finger touched my lips, and she sighed, before smiling slightly. "Does it matter if it was? When the person I chose is you?"

Did she really want me?

I gripped her hand and kissed the tip of that finger, and then the next, and the next.

It didn't matter.

Even if she was only with me to monitor me.

Even if it was out of pity, she still chose me.

That's all that matters, right?

I had to think about that else before I sink again.

I sucked on the tip of her index finger, giving a slight bite and shuddering at the moan that escaped her lips. When I finally let go, her lips were back on mine and my god. The kiss was sloppier and needier than before. Was it because of the anger? The jealousy?

Or just desire between two broken strangers desperate for the closest connection imaginable?

Cause I remembered... she was broken, too.

We would've died together.

My lips pulled back from hers and I pulled off my shirt, grateful that the shadows of the night covered the thousands of scars that littered my ribs and stomach. Another thing that would've drowned me if it wasn't because she was kissing my chest and nibbling on my neck and collarbone. I groaned and grasped at her blouse again, pulling it up. If she didn't lean back, I would've torn it off while whispering sorry.

I didn't want to say sorry.

I wanted... I wanted to say something else. "Your-your name. Can... Can you tell me your name?"

She was flushed; rose red coloring her cheeks and noses, her plump lips, swollen from our eager kisses, parted, "Ma-Mallena..."

Mallena...

Mallena...

That's what I wanted to say. Her name. I needed it on my lips. "Mallena... you're so beautiful... I... I'm rusty at this, but I-I really want you."

She panted softly and then gave me that enigmatic smile. "I want you too... Mr. Rooftop."

I guffawed and snorted, nuzzling against her bare shoulder before nibbling her neck. "Cole... my name is Cole, Mallena."

Chapter Six
A Lonely Morning

This was new.

Okay, not new.

This was unfamiliar.

I opened my eyes before needing to shut them immediately.

It was so bright.

Did... did I sleep through the night?

Well... most of the night?

I groaned, pressing my head against the fluffy pillow before lifting my head up and suddenly staring at the ivory cushion.

This was not my pillow.

My pillow was not so soft.

I pressed my palms against the bed and pushed myself up.

Yup.

This was not my bed either.

Sitting back on my heels, I rubbed my neck. My mouth stretched open as I yawned and took in my surroundings.

Ivory and white sheets with matching comforter and pillows.

Blackout curtains that were slightly opened to let in the morning light.

A small built-in desk next to a large LED tv on top of a brown nondescript set of drawers.

A used condom next to my hand-

... What?

My hand lurched away, and I scrambled to the headboard.

I ran my other hand down from my forehead to my mouth, staring at the sticky used condom. My ears are burning and I realized another very important fact.

I was completely naked.

I chewed on my cheek, blood rushing to my cheeks and my dick. My hand lowered to the sheets, gripping them tightly as I remember the night before.

Mallena.

From her name, more memories flooded back. "Mallena..."

Those starry eyes staring into mine, her arms wrapping around my neck to pull me close. Her legs locked around my hips and god the sounds. Her sounds and her taste. I must've been so awkward, but when she lowered my head between her thighs, I knew that this was not just a night for me.

It was for her.

For us.

I... I think I fell in love.

I lifted my hands and slammed my palms against my cheeks.

Stop it.

Stop getting ahead of yourself.

I only knew her for one crazy, heavenly night.

I knew nothing about her.

I only knew her first name and who knows if it's her actual name. It could've been fake.

Yet the peace I felt being with her, cuddling her, sharing a bed, sharing the same air.

I wanted that again.

It would be unfair, though. To just shove all of my needs and expectations on her. Even I knew that.

Yet, if I could just ask her for another time. A date, or even a coffee after we deal with this awkward morning, that would be enough.

At least having her in my life would motivate me to pull the jagged pieces of myself out of the void and back together again.

Somehow.

... Where was she?

I looked around, my cheeks stinging from the slap. She wasn't next to me and I didn't hear the shower. I throw my legs over the edge of the bed and pull up my boxers. My fingers took a moment to the rough lines and patches on my stomach and chest.

It was so dark when we stripped each other and we were too busy making a mess of each other focus on our flaws-

Ours?

Bullshit.

She's gorgeous.

Her skin was smooth and flawless.

Her sweat tasted sweet and her skin shimmered like copper.

Nothing about her was less than perfect.

So maybe it was me.

Maybe she saw how my skin reflected my broken mind... and it disgusted her.

I could feel the knot forming in the center of my head and radiate outwards. The weight, the fog, it was coming back.

She was ashamed to stay.

You were coyote ugly. If she stayed, she would've gnawed off her arms to get away from you.

You're a piece of shit.

She could have anyone in the world and all she got was you.

"Does it matter if it was? When the person I chose is you?"

I wanted to believe that. I wanted to hold on to that. Even if she didn't mean it, my brain was starving for anything it could hold on to.

God, why did she leave?

My grasp on that hope was slipping, and that I was depending on just one night to move forward is adding another brick onto my back.

I'm Atlas's insignificant mortal counter pointer and instead of carrying the world, I carry the pointless sham that is myself.

My right hand clenched to a fist and I press it against my forehead, hitting the same painful knot repeatedly. I tried doing this before. Tried so hard to beat the agonizing truth out of my head and just like before; I am failing and falling.

I gritted my teeth and shuddered, choking on a sob as I leaned against the headboard, my arms stretched out to the side, staring at the ceiling.

Bland and empty.

Just like me.

My eyes shift from the ceiling towards the drawers that were on her side.

There was a paper there, just pinned underneath the phone. I grimaced, feeling hope rising. I was only going to be disappointed.

I could've sworn every single part of my being knew that.

Yet there it was.

Hope.

Hope that the piece of paper wasn't just a room service menu.

A list of channels.

The Wi-Fi password.

A bill.

Hope that it would be in her handwriting, even though I did not know what her handwriting looked like.

Whatever it was, just please let it be from her.

Fear and hope kept fighting and warring with each other as I pressed my knees against my chest, my head burrowing into my forearms. I was shaking and my heart was stabbing itself into my ribs.

Hope.

Fear.

Please be from her.

I was begging to whatever cruel omnipotent asshole listening.

Let it be her.

A chill crawls up my spine and made me shake.

Fuck it.

Look at it.

Just like ripping off a bandaid.

I lifted my head and move one hand over to the nightstand. Time slowed down as my fingertips pause just above the letter.

Fear.

Hope.

Mallena.

Why did you leave?

I picked up the paper and lift it up.

As I brought it closer, I realized it smells like her.

A scent of roses growing in an ancient forest and yes, I was aware of how fucking stupid that sounded, but I swear to omnipotent asshole that is her scent and that is what the paper smelled like.

I brought the letter up to eye level and time went back to normal.

All I had to do was shut up the void enough to read it.

Chapter Seven
I'm Sorry

Good morning, Cole.

It's one syllable.

One fucking syllable.

I told her my name yesterday and while we were busy, I'm sure it's easy to remember.

Yet, I was smiling. This could be One-Night Stand equivalent of a 'Dear John' letter, but my name was important enough to remember.

Pathetic.

I'm sorry that I couldn't stay longer. I really enjoyed last night, and I was tempted to have a fun morning for you. But I couldn't stay. That wouldn't have good for you and I like you too much.

... huh?

I'm sure I would've loved morning sex.

A chill slithered up my spine.

I lowered the letter for a few moments and patted down my sides.

Nope, just old scars. No new stitches.

I used a condom, so I was still STD-free...okay a check up wouldn't hurt...

I shook my head, trying to ignore the paranoia fog summoned by the void.

My eyes returned to the letter.

If you worried about your liver or kidneys from that urban legend, I hope you realize that I'm not that kind of person and I mean it. I really do like you.

The room is paid for the next three nights. I didn't know if you had a place to stay and I don't want you out in the cold. I also left a paid tab for you so you can order some food.

I know you can take care of yourself.

I also know that you're not okay.

The knot returned, and my shoulders sagged.

It was so obvious that I was not okay.

I just wished that it didn't hurt so much to see it in writing.

I wondered if she thought my body was just as broken as my mind.

... Well, she still liked me enough for a long emotional cuddle and passionate sex, so hurray?

Please take care of yourself, Cole.

I don't know if I'll see you again. I hope I do. That doesn't mean much, but I really hope I do.

I looked over at the cold side of the bed; she was so small and warm in my arms. I think I fell asleep kissing her repeatedly, her gentle giggles and sighs a lullaby.

God, why did she leave?

I hope that you're alive. I hope you stay alive. So the chances that we see each other again are not zero. I want you to stay alive, Cole. Because that means that I can see you again. Maybe go for another round?

Of drinks?

Or of sex?

Both.

Would she want me enough for both?

So for that one hypothetical future night, be alive and well, Cole.

Be alive and well.

Hoping to see you later,

Mallena.

She wanted to see me again... but didn't leave her number.

All I have of her was this letter, coated in her perfume, her handwriting, her name, and last night.

Hope.

Fear.

Fuck off Fear.

Let me have hope!

I grabbed onto it, burrowing it into my chest like I wanted it tattooed on my chest. Just so I can read it every single day of my life.

Did she want to see me? Did she just say that to manipulate me into continuing my piece of shit life?

"Does it matter, when I chose you?"

No, no, it didn't matter.

I want to see her again.

To see her... I... I need to live.

I need to live somehow and keep the void at bay.

Fuck... I need help.

I need so much goddamn help.

"I... I want to see you, Mallena. For some hypothetical night... I want to see you."

I fell in love... I don't even know if I'll ever see her again but...

I will.

For that, I need to live.

I shuddered, taking slow breaths as I tried to piece my life back together in my head.

Step by step. Piece by piece.

Build up the shambles and try, just try to make it work somehow.

I ran one hand through my hair, scratching my scalp before tugging at the oily locks.

How?

How do I go about this?

It's too much. Too much weight. How many friendships have I thrown away? All the pills have I flushed down the drain because my stomach hated them or my motivation, already a rare resource, died. All the fist fights I had with my brothers after a shit-faced night.

Did I have anyone to help shoulder this?

... I did.

God, I haven't talked to them in over a year.

I looked over to the hotel phone. I had foregone getting a cell phone. Well, more like I kept breaking them, or flushing them down the toilet during my many bouts with my suffocating mind. I had wandered so long and so lost in the fog that there was only one answer left.

"I would be sad if you died."
"You don't know me."
"Yet I care enough to save your life, right?"

I have to see her again. For at least the smallest chance of that...

I have to live.

I swallowed, whimpering as a familiar 10 digit number repeated in my head. A sequence of nostalgic digits dancing just above the void that wanted to devour them.

Wanted to devour me.

I turned over to the nightstand and picked up the phone.

My index finger poised over the first number as I pressed the receiver against my ear.

Would they still have this number?

What if they gave up on the landline?

What if they moved?

God, are they even together?

Are they alive?

What if... what I speak... and they hung up?

They must've given up on me.

I moved the phone away, my shoulders leaning over. A thick, hazy weight pushed me down... down...

"Hey... come back."

I gritted my teeth. Everything was so heavy, and the air was thick, but I had to do this. I have to live.

I pressed my finger on the first digit, then the other, and another.

The void is trying to dig its smoking tendrils into me.

Fuck off!

My hand jerked away from the touchpad as if it was burning lava. The dial-tone began, and I gulped, my heart almost stopping.

A click.

Someone, somehow, picked up.

"Hello? Jenna Holton speaking?"

I chewed on my inner cheek, biting so hard, a tint of copper touched my tongue.

"Hello?... Hello?... Gene I don't know, no one's answering-"

I could hear another voice in the background and I whimpered at the irritation in her voice. My lip bottom lip quivered, and I stopped being a chickenshit, "M-mom..."

"... Cole? Oh-Oh my god. Cole, baby, is that you?"

She... she didn't hang up.

She didn't give up on me.

"Oh god. Gene! GENE! It's Cole! He called, he finally called!" The excitement in her voice was tempered by the distinctive waver in her tone. She was about to cry.

I made my mother cry.

Loud steps hurried towards the foreground and the deep baritone of my father leapt from the receiver and into my ears, "Cole! Thank god... for fuck's sake's son! Jesus Christ, where have you been?! We thought... I thought you... oh god... my son is alive... our son is alive!"

Oh no, his voice wavering too.

Fuck...

I wiped my eyes, shoulders shaking, "Y-yeah... hey m-mom. Hey dad... I'm... I'm alive... I... I'll be home soon."

Chapter Eight
New Lease on Life

I looked at the orange bottle and sighed. Already my stomach was curling in on itself, begging me not to take it.

Sorry stomach.

You'll have to suffer another day.

I shook two tablets out of the bottle, holding them in one hand while gripping the tumbler in another.

Don't worry.

I'll make it quick.

I shoved the pills into my mouth, followed by chugging the entire cup of water. I swallowed heavily, turning on the faucet to splash water against my face.

I am still alive.

Honestly, not that bad. The nausea was so much worse when I took my first dose, and it was becoming more of a nuisance than a porcelain throne hugging disaster. Even when the 200 milligrams beat the living shit out of my stomach (literally, unfortunately), the void was kept at bay.

Sort of.

It was still there. Still roiling in the back of my head, a dull throb that twitched every time my anxiety got the best of me.

It nearly got me again when I stood in front of my parent's door, my knuckles millimeters from the woods, but suffocating doubt tightened like a noose around my neck and I could not breathe. I was choking on my spit and fear, frozen in place.

If it wasn't for my mom coming from the garden, I probably would've just walked towards the nearest highway and jump right in front of a semi.

Leaving behind only disappointment and regret.

I would've thrown away my chance to see Mallena again.

I shook my head, water splashing against the ivory clamshell sink. I grabbed face towel and wiped off the remaining fluid from my forehead and eyes, setting the fabric against the sink before opening the door, "Ugh, mom, I thought you and dad escaped the 80s."

"Well, we couldn't decide on what style." My mother's raspy voice traveled from her desk, greeting me as I entered the den. She spun her chair around, almost skipping in front of the tv before hugging me close.

I have been here for half a month and she was still hugging me.

"Down in front!" Dad tilted his head to the side, scowling. "Trying to watch the game here!"

"Okay, Gene, first off, it's baseball and I know you don't give a damn! Second, I am giving my son his three time's a day hug!"

I couldn't get a word in edge-wise as she squeezed even tighter. I swear the woman is nearing 55 yet she felt as strong as she did when I was just a kid and skinned my knee.

She was still as strong as a grizzly bear.

"All right, if you two won't get down, I'll have to drag you down!" Two enormous arms, with graying hairs, wrapped around us, knocking out whatever air I had left in my lungs. With a hefty huff, Dad fell back onto the couch, dragging us down with him.

I'm sorry, Mallena.

My parents are going to kill me first.

"Gene!" My mom coughed, the sudden impact winding her. She pushed off of me, freeing herself and leaving her son to suffer.

Thanks mom.

My dad laughed, and his grip loosened just enough so I can get some oxygen in me. However, he still held me firm, his laugh fading into silence.

I closed my eyes as he shuddered and patted his back. "Dad, did you get jealous of mom?"

He chuckled; it was a deep rumbling sound that came from his gut. He pulled back, letting me get up so I can sit next to him.

I couldn't look at him and when I heard that shivering breath from my mom, I couldn't look at her either. "G-guys, come on... I'm still here."

A heavy thud almost knocked me forward as Dad patted my back. His hands felt just as big as they did when he threw me in the air back when I was a toddler. I took a deep breath and turned my head, just so I can see him nod in my periphery. "I know, son. It's just... it's good to have you here."

Mom was silent, sitting on the other side of me and patting my knee. I could hear her sniffling a little before she grunted. "Yeah, and you're going to be staying here." She cleared her throat, "As long as you need to."

My lips twitched just a little. "I know. Thanks, guys."

Chapter Nine
Session Z

My knees fidgeted and my clammy fingers struggled to keep them still.

This was my sixth appointment with my therapist, and I still shake like a fucking leaf.

It wasn't like I didn't like the guy.

He was like me.

Hell, maybe worse off! The guy was missing a fucking arm, for god's sake.

"I can't confirm the existence of any W.M.Ds." He leaned forward, round glasses sliding down his nose, "I can confirm that this hurt like a son of a bitch."

That candidness I appreciated.

It reminded me of you, Mallena.

The problem was that he wasn't you.

My parents weren't you.

They were all echoes of the void, speaking into the back of my mind. Vitamin Z turned the shouts into whispers, but the mantra remained.

The scars I hide underneath long sleeve shirts, flannels and jackets, no one has seen.

No one but you.

I'm not sure you even seen them.

I blinked, hearing a clink of glass settling on the coffee table between me and the therapist. He sat back down, a relaxed smile on his face.

Sometimes we wouldn't speak at all.

He wouldn't force it. He already knew that it was an enormous feat for me to come here. My parents, despite the hellish year I put them through, didn't force me to speak about why I stayed so fucking broken.

Before I came back from deployment, I had shattered into a million pieces and since then have been failing at putting the pieces in place.

I picked up the glass and took a shaky sip, my head lowered so I wouldn't imagine the gaze of disappointment in his eyes. "So-sorry."

"Don't be. This is your time. You know I am content with letting you settle in and take the hour to yourself. The only thing I care about is that you leave here feeling a little better than you came in."

I swallowed and nodded, setting the glass done. "I appreciate that, Sir..."

"We're retired now, civilians."

"I know, I just feel comfortable calling you that."

His chuckle was a deep bass, like the purr of a cat. A big, wise cat. He didn't push the issue and leaned forward. His left ankle settled on his right knee. "I assume that something is on your mind today?"

I nodded, looking out the window, "I'm... I'm thinking about getting a job. I'm not sure what kind of job yet. Since you're my therapist, maybe we can talk through some options?"

He nodded; as if that was what he expected all along. A sort of nod that anyone leaner and younger would seem condescending, yet on him, it was a wise movement of an experienced sage, "Of course." He sat up and rubbed his chin, the gray curls of his beard rustling, "This is quite the step and while I am no career counselor, you had a hard time since your service."

Hard time?

No.

A hellish nightmare torment time?

Yes.

My hand gripped my knee, fingers digging in to stop the jerking. The sudden clamp made my leg stiffen, vibrating jolts running up against the bone.

God, I hated how he noticed. His side tilted just to the side, his cheeks plump as he gave a smile worthy of Santa Claus, "How is the Zoloft treating you, Cole?"

"Fine." Not completely fine; the void could no longer wrap its viscous tar tentacles around my brain and leech off my serotonin, but it was still there. Waiting patiently; the nausea would pass and I would grow complacent.

Then it would feast.

I will not be complacent. I will not let it feed.

I am getting better; I am getting help.

I also needed to get stable.

"Is there something you are thinking of doing?"

The finality of my 'Fine' must've told him it was time to move on from my meds. "I'm not sure... I wasn't able to finish my courses during my term."

"You are entitled to tuition through the GI Bill. You were studying Civil Engineering, right? Think about transferring credits."

I chewed on my bottom lip. He made it sound so simple. That was the problem. They all made it sound so simple, "Y-yeah, my parents... they said the same thing." It was so hard picking up the phone to call mom. Did they think it would be easy to call up a stranger about college? How would I even start? How many colleges would accept me. Would I have to describe why I quit? I couldn't cut it? That the buildings I wanted to build were the same ones that exploded? Shrapnel cutting into my face and dust filling my lungs? That I couldn't fucking focus anymore?!

You chickened out, chicken shit.

I closed my eyes and as soon as my hand left my knee; it shook as if there was an earthquake directly under the soles of my feet. "I'm not sure about taking classes right now. Even if I planned on it... I don't want to keep living with my parents. Especially when there is someone I want to see again."

"Mallena, huh? I need to thank her for getting you here." He paused, and I didn't look up. It was so much easier to stare at my bouncing leg. I glared at it, hating how it moved. Here I was feeling sorry for myself and this guy, this DOCTOR, is missing an arm from Iraq and I... god now I'm using guilt to feed into my anxiety.

At least I recognized that.

"Cole, is there something you've been enjoying? I know you are living with your parents, which is normal by the way."

He cut off that bit of guilt before it could bite down.

"You told me you've been helping around the house? Anything that sparked your interest. It's good you want to earn a living, so choose something that invigorates you while supporting your wellbeing."

My wellbeing...?

I turned my hands up, staring at my palms. I thought back to mom and that garden. She started that just recently. Bending down with a small trowel, digging into the espresso dirt. I sat down onto the tawny cobblestone terrace wall, watching as she set the trowel on the ground and with her thin, yellow gloves, daintily mold a small clean hole. The sun blanketed us with a peaceful warmth as she placed a bulb in that hole. With the same amount of gentle care, she scooped the earth over the bulb, tucking it into the earth.

I turned my head to watch my dad work the shears. His task was not nearly so delicate, yet he was poised, trimming the stray leaves and branches of the rose bushes like a sculptor, chiseling off an unnecessary piece in order to give the plants new life and comfort.

When I had asked to help, both of them looked back at me, and they each smiled, before playfully arguing who got their son's free labor first.

Seeing the little callouses on my hands while watering the blossoming bulbs made me think of you.

I always wanted to build. I always wanted to plant.

I wanted to bring life into something.

Instead of taking it away, until I was ripping into my skin, tearing chunks of my disgusting self out into the trash where I belonged.

I blinked back into the office, looking at Santa Claus dressed in the warm tan and peach suit of my therapist, "... I... I enjoy gardening. Being outside... I think I want to keep doing that..."

Chapter Ten
The Manor

"See that?" Mr. Martinez pointed out the window, his arm crossing over his chest as his eyes focused on the road. "See that cliff side. How the edge just keeps stretching out and out, even though you'd think the tip will break off like in one of those Coyote cartoons? We call it The Dick de Milagro."

I coughed sharply when the back of his hand hit my chest. Fuck for 55, he knew how to knock the wind out of my lungs, "Mr. Martinez, my folks took me through these roads since I was born and I know no one calls it that."

"Okay, well I call it that because only a dick can get that hard and stick out so far without falling."

I rolled my eyes, looking behind me towards the truck following us, "I hope Ricky doesn't believe your bullshit."

"My son believes whatever I pay him to believe, thus that is El Dick de Milagro."

Yes, this man was the epitome of professionalism.

At the advice of my therapist, and once I grew some balls, I went to a group session specifically for veterans. I was sitting in between a helicopter pilot who lost an eye and a sergeant who lost both legs stepping on an IED. The worst part was being late and walking in on the middle of a Doc talking about a dream he kept having; a dream of holding a little girl in his arms, half her head blown off.

The void reminded me of how good I had it compared to these authentic heroes. All I had was a fucked up brain and a shredded up body. These men around made real sacrifices, and I was a fake, an imposter—

I lowered my head down to my feet, grasping at my backpack and sighing in relief as the orange bottle of Vitamin Z glittered back at me. Did I take my dose? I thought I did, but we've been driving for so long, going up and down hills, through dense trees that I had forgotten. Which is exactly what a piece of shit like me would do—

"Cole. Bro. You disappearing again."

"Hey... Come back to me..."

I shuddered, shaking my head and once I dropped my pack between my feet, I shook out the shakes from my fingers as well, "Y-Yeah... I just... I just can't remember if I took my pills."

"Yeah, Ricky and Chucky watched you this morning. You're okay brother." Mr. Martinez glanced at me, his lips lifting at the corners as he nodded, "You need to talk, I can listen."

A chuckle escaped my lips before I can stop it. "You like hearing your voice too much, Sir."

"Shithead."

The pills, my parents, this job... they help keep the void quelled and quiet. I can look in the mirror and see myself without wanting to throw up at the sight. The group session... I didn't talk much cause I mean, even though we all been through some shit, they were still all strangers.

None of my brothers actually came home.

So, how could I talk?

No one forced me, not even the retired Colonel leading the session, her plastic and metal arm left arm folded on her lap as she listened to our stories, her right hand holding a cup of coffee, which she reminded we were all welcomed to.

Most of the younger guys, like me, we kept a little quiet, some of us just checking the mood of the group.

The older guys, they were more open; one dude in a cowboy hat talked about his time in Vietnam, while another who reminded me of my grandpa, talked about losing an arm in Korea, his heavily accented voice describing coming off the plane from San Juan only to lose his right arm on the bus ride after. A few of us laughed, though no one laughed as hard as Mr. Martinez.

I think that's when I felt relaxed enough to get my head out of my ass. Hearing this whacky Marine laugh at an 84-year-old Master Sergeant who lost his arm via collision with a pole during a bus ride just brought me up from hell and onto Earth. The one armed grandpa was laughing as well, pointing out that at least he didn't lose a leg losing a bet at a bar in Saudi Arabia. I don't know how much of this back and forth was all bullshit, but Mr. Martinez had a cheeky glint of life in his eyes.

When the main session was over and we were all just shooting the shit, away from the heavy crap the old vets talked about and younger ones absorbed. The cowboy and Mr. Martinez chatted about bored housewives and soccer moms micromanaging on how many millimeters their hedges need to be trimmed and whether a Japanese tea garden can have English roses and still be 'authentic' (his old south accent was really thick, I had to listen in), than actually talking landscaping.

Once the tirade and venting was complete, Mr. Martinez talked about how he prefers to take jobs in the mountains for that reason: mostly old historical homes, mining facilities and related rock work, and much larger land area, which meant more labor and more money. Also meant less people.

"I'd like to garden..."

The idea of working on trimming tree branches, clearing boulders from roads while taking in the sights of hills and mountains, isolated from voices that could feed into the void, attracted me. Once the cowboy left and it was just me, I worked my balls again for one more miracle and asked Mr. Martinez for a job.

Which leads me to being trapped in a car for the past 3 hours with an Ex-Marine talking about Dick Cliffs.

Life finds a way.

"Look out there." A deeply tanned and calloused finger cut across my view, pointing out the window. I was about to quip about keeping his ass scratching digits out of my face before my eyes shifted to the side.

Holy shit.

The trees opened up, revealing crystal blue waters sparkling with the sun on the surface. Several willows bowed in reverence towards the solitary but enchanting body of water; their leaves dangled and danced like swirling braids against the surface. Protective pines guarded circled the lake and stood stoically like a fence in front of a mansion looming in the distance.

The mountains grew from behind that solitary manor, the building and majestic peaks reflecting over the sparkling lake. The dense forest cover returned as we drove closer to the property; pass the wooden and barbed wire gate, ominously holding a 'Private Property' sign, the dirt road turned into gravel. Mr. Martinez was unusually silent despite several guffaws. I'm sure he was laughing at my stupid, gaping face.

I have lived here a LONG time, and yet never even heard of this lake or this manor. In this day of age of google searches and directory listings of hiking trails, this was a private and hidden gem, "There's...no one's here."

"That's not true. Look at Kenneth over there."

I blinked as our small caravans carrying mini excavators, skid steer loaders, and the odd ride on a mower or two slowed to a stop. Mr. Martinez parked the wagon. We were in front of another gate, metal bars, with a red STOP sign prevented our passing.

As my boss lowered his window, a heavily bearded man with Paul Bunyan shoulders stepped out of the guardhouse. He even picked up an axe behind his back, marching with the gait of a slasher and charm of a lumberjack.

This must be Kenneth.

"Angel, you got your contract renewed?" The linebacker-size guard with the Santa Claus beard bent down to look eye to eye with Mr. Martinez, grey eyes glittering with familiarity. I couldn't see it, but I assumed somewhere under that waterfall of hair was a smile.

"Kenny! You know it, man. Your boss, she can't get enough of me."

Kenneth's eyes glittered like Santa Claus, though I flinched as he hoisted that axe and rested the handle on his shoulders. "She doesn't have many options! You and your boys are the only idiots willing to come round here."

Seriously?

I blinked and looked out my window again.

Lush green trees.

Hilly trails edged with rich bushes?

A lake with large willow trees, providing shade, less than a quarter mile away?

Why would no one else come here?

Why was this not teeming with trespassing tourists?!

I turned my head towards my boss's window and took in that axe again.

When someone in the size of a shaved bigfoot, wielding an axe, is a guard here, maybe trespassing wasn't a fun idea.

"Oh hey Kenny, got some new blood."

I turned my head just enough for the axe to stay in the periphery of my vision, "Cole Holton, sir."

Kenneth nodded, though his moustache lowered, "Welcome, Cole." He nodded his head, but the sparkle left his eyes as he turned his attention to Mr. Martinez, "Sabina knows about the new guy?"

"Nah, I'm just gonna surprise her with some new eye candy."

I would've at least smirked if not for the icy glare leveled towards my boss from Kenneth, who suddenly looked less like St. Nick and more like Michael Myers bearded uncle. Mr. 'Dick De Milagro' was not perturbed. "Hey man, I talked to your boss. She is gonna meet us at the palace, no problem."

My shoulders hunched as those silver eyes stared at me from under bushy grey eyebrows. My hands were a lot more interesting at the moment.

Shit, I can see my wrists peeking through.

Besides the short shrapnel scars, I can also count the lines on top of the joint. Some lines were shallow streams of pink and white, others were deeper, searing across closed veins and rotten arteries.

One, two, Christ, five...

Going up my arm. I fought the urge to lift my sleeve, instead my hand rubbed the edge of the flannel against my wrist. Was the air always so thick? My ears popped and fill with fluid.

Was I drowning?

Deep bass voices floated by, distorted and growing lower in pitch.

Lower.

And lower.

Until I heard nothing but vibrating growls.

The void opened its mouth wide. Its vortex was sucking me in. I am a piece of dirt being vacuumed into nothingness.

My eyes snapped open as my body jerked forward, the car coming back to life under my feet. I swallowed heavily, my throat dry and raw as I looked towards Mr. Martinez.

His eyes stayed forward, but he still had that carefree smirk on his face. "Kenny's a good guy. Scary, but once his boss got the radio, he went all soft."

I got my lips to twist upwards in some kind of smile, which earned me a pat on the shoulder. I don't think the forced smile worked; he patted me out of pity, not even glancing at my stretched muscles. I looked away from him, letting the mask fall.

I was the new guy and seeing Kenny and this 'Sabina', I am a nobody.

I'll have to prove myself.

My stomach twisted itself into knots; knot with mouths that opened with jagged teeth, gnawing into itself. My arms curled over my belly and I faced my feet, forcing my eyes open and yet unwilling to look out the window just yet.

The car stopped again. Mr. Martinez patted my shoulder again, this time gripping it firmly. "You got this, Cole. I wanted you here because this contract is private. No crazy soccer moms or lawyers with their heads stuck all the way up their culo." When I turned my head to look up at him, his lips curled down just at the edges. "I ain't gonna lie. Sabina can be a hardass. You can have the greenest thumbs, but you act stupid or she doesn't like you. I'm dragging your ass back, okay?"

I shuddered, sitting up straight, watching the large black iron gates open, inch by slow inch. This was a warning, but also a reprieve.

If things got too hard, Mr. Martinez would get me home. He wasn't saying he fired me.

He was a way out.

I nodded, my lips pursing as we drove through the gate; stone gargoyles choked by thorny vines stared down at us as we made our ways towards the manor.

Chapter Eleven
The Housekeeper

The voracious void in my stomach, was satisfied, but when we parked just to the side of the intimidating, Notre Dame styled gate, Ricky and Chuck in the truck next to us, I had to fight the urge to puke again.

There was something about this place that felt...wrong. It wasn't just the lumberjack who could switch from Santa Claus to the bearded Terminator in two seconds. It wasn't just this secretive mysterious Sabina who could make Mr. Martinez dismiss me if I looked at her wrong.

It was the gargoyles staring at us, watching us as we opened our doors and placed our feet onto sacred ground. The serene lake sparkled behind towering trees connected by thorny vines wrapped possessively around the trunks; roots rolled under the sweeping cobblestone driveway that swirled again and again, spiraling towards a black gazebo with iron columns, made of vines wrapping around each other, topped with a gold plated dome. The ironwork seemed to writhe, the vines around the columns clawing onto the roofing, intertwining to make a spire at the top. I narrowed my eyes to glance closer at the gothic structure; these mountains held plenty of Victorian cabins; gingerbread like structures that painted the browns and greens elevations with painted reds, yellows, and other pastel shades.

This central thing in the driveway, the courtyard to better describe it, felt older and foreboding. The columns, black with sharp protrusions similar to the thorny vines twisting around the trees, would definitely not be found near any gingerbread house.

The gate, the fortress, seemed to judge me. It found me wanting.

It was as if the void that tore into my psyche suddenly had an external form. I felt exceedingly unwelcomed here.

I felt the same way in my skin.

"I hate coming here either, bro." Ricky released a heavy sigh; his face would be a dead ringer for Mr. Martinez if it wasn't for the lack of wrinkles and lower set brow. He always looked as if he was perpetually glaring and this was no different. In fact, his thick eyebrows seem to sink even lower, hiding the top lids of his brown eyes. "Place always gives me the creeps."

Mr. Martinez stepped out of his SUV and even his normal jovial grin was...forced, "A regular contract that pays brings in plenty of cash and no competition." It was as if he was almost psyching himself up, "A golden goose, or unicorn contract." He turned his head over to Chuck, who I could hear unloading the mower and weed eaters. Mr. Martinez kept his eyes away from the creepy gazebo and gargoyle fortified gate. "Ricardo, no scaring Cole."

Ricky snorted, rolling his eyes. "I give him a week, tops. If he lasts, I buy a round of tequila. We are gonna need it after this season."

Ricky was always more brusque than his father, so I expected the cynicism. However, the heavy shadow over his eyes made me realize he was serious.

I swallowed heavily, wiping some sweat under my chin. It was still morning, only 65 degrees, yet there was no breeze. So rustling of leaves.

No life.

Ricky nudged my shoulder with his, motioning over to the quiet Chuck carrying two weed eaters. Mr. Martinez was already riding the mower. I nodded, knots rolling under my skin as I moved to the truck, grabbing the hoses while Ricky rolled the wheelbarrow with fertilizer.

Such a strange place, frozen in time, yet lush with iron like vines. In an uncomfortable silence, we walked across the driveway, towards the pavilion connected to the ancient manor.

I could only describe it as ancient; leafy vines covered the wood and brick walls. They climbed like fingers up the towers and even onto tented roofs covered by onyx slate with gold filigree. My eyes scanned over the walls, seeing pink and peach of the exterior peaking from under the greenery before the sudden burst of color caught my eye. A swirl of mosaic tile in blues, reds, and golds captured my gaze and, unlike the possessive vines, the cyclic pattern teased my vision, playfully weaving throughout the stone and up towards that window.

I was entranced, following those colors; how could something so bright and joyful peek out from a foreboding place? It welcomed my stare, coaxing it higher and higher. The colors became bright in shades as they escaped from the shade and glistened in the sunlight.

At the top of their playful flight, the sparkle of metal and glass danced around a round balcony. I backed up, curiosity taking a hold of my feet and coaxing me back just enough to get a view of what was at the top.

A window.

A large, arched window with iron panes and a curtain blocking all from looking in and looking out.

"Huh..."

The wonder gave way to disappointment. A feeling I am very much used to, yet was also plagued by questions.

Why would thick curtains cover such a large window that was surrounded by fairies of light? Surely the owner would use this spot to admire their private lake and the surrounding mountains? It was a waste to keep it blocked.

I backed up further and then froze.

The curtain seemed to shift slightly, letting the tiniest amount of light to sneak in.

I can't explain why but my it belt like two walls fell on either side of me, blocking distractions in my periphery. My head throbbed, staring at that tiny slit through the curtain. The window didn't open; the balcony remained empty, but the longer I stared at that tiny opening, the more pressure fell on me. I tried to pick up my feet, but they sunk into the ground. I tried to turn my head, but the walls closed in; the only light I could see at that window.

No, no, the window.

That fluttering slit of the curtain.

Was it always so hot?

The fairy lights were no longer playful. They didn't dance.

They flicked and turned into burning embers, pounding at the balcony. Smoke filled the air. Black smoke filled my senses and I couldn't breathe.

I blinked, but my eyes were dry. There was no moisture in the air.

My chest felt tight and my throat closed in. I tasted goal and ash coated my tongue. The embers fell onto me and they burned holes into my flesh. Tiny cigarette burns covering me, inch by inch.

I wanted to scream, but my voice was raspy and my esophagus was scrubbed raw by the black soot and ash. This wasn't the void; I wasn't drowning under a flood of nothingness.

No, I was burning.

I was burning alive.

The air was crackling around me, and I was melting into the mud.

Then cold fingers grasped my upper arm, squeezing tightly, ice filling my veins. "What are you doing?"

The walls collapsed, the smoke receded. The embers turned back into rainbow refractions dancing around the balcony.

I could breathe again. When I swallowed, I tasted my drool, mucus, and a bit of vomit that I almost threw up onto the dirt.

The only thing that remained was the throbbing in my skull and the pounding of my heart.

The cold vanished, the freezing ice left my skin, leaving only chilled sweat.

"I said, 'What are you doing?'"

The voice was sharp and acidic and I could creak my neck to the side.

Dark eyes; almost black in shade, stared back. No light could be found in that cold gaze, just the vast blackness of space.

Word failed me, and I gaped, looking up towards the balcony again. "Stop."

Her voice lashed out like a whip and I looked back at her, clutching my shirt over my heart, trying to make it stop, "I...I saw...I thought..."

"You saw nothing." That hiss made the rest of her features came into view. She was pale; there was no color on his skin. No pinks, yellows, or blues, nothing but a pale, dead gray. Her straight hair, just as lifeless, did not sparkle in the sunlight; it laid against her face like bone.

I could only stare, gaping like a fish out of water.

"Senora!" Mr. Martinez snuck up to my side, making me jump as his hand clasped my shoulder, "I see you met my newest guy!" He gave the grey woman a disarming grin, squeezing my shoulder not only to ease the knots in my muscles but also to stop me from falling apart, "This place is so big, it's easy to get lost."

The woman's coal-black eyes narrowed into slits so thin the whites of her eyes could no longer be seen. "Martinez, what are the rules."

The calloused hand on my shoulder trembled. I looked over at Mr. Martinez's face, watching as that grin slowly faded. "Senora, we only just arrived."

The trepidation in his voice made my eyes fall into the dirt and pavement, watching a worm squirm between the cracks.

I was watching myself squirm.

"Yet here he was, sneaking around. Like a rat." That thin slit glare stayed on me; the nothingness in those horizontal alley eyes seemed to suck out all life from my limbs. "I was expecting your crew to be in the gardens, not scoping out entrances so blatantly."

Before Mr. Martinez could speak, I managed out a raspy whisper. My throat still hurt like hell. "I wasn't scoping. I saw s-something b-burn-"

"You saw nothing." Her chilly voice sent doubts about the heat I had felt, the tunnel vision, the absolute horror I had just experienced.

You are losing it again, Cole.

Absolute piece of shit person.

A rat seeing things and scavenging remains of pity; what am I putting Mr. Martinez through?

His hand moved from my shoulder and he rubbed the back of his neck, "I will make sure he follows your guidelines, Senora Sabina."

So the woman who watched out of a silent film, no color or warmth in her face nor her voice, was the client. The lady of the house and I was a thief.

Fuck, I am useless.

"I can't trust you to do that, can I?" Her voice was as sharp as always, slicing through my boss' concession. Yet not once did she look at him? I can tell.

Her gaze, as empty as a black-hole, was feeding into the void.

"I have rules to give to anyone who working here." The edge of her eyes dulled, becoming flat, echoing through my ears. The contract between the client and contract turned into an oath of which any breach was a betrayal most grave.

Even Mr. Martinez was silent at Sabina's solemn words.

"One: you must never look into the manor during the day. You are to work outside." Her hand motioned towards the side courtyards, "Shade and cover are freely available so do not seek shelter here."

Her hand lowered, "Two: NEVER ENTER THE MANOR DURING THE DAY."

I looked up; blinking.

This place was gigantic. The manor must be labyrinthian.

Yet our trucks were the only ones I saw parked.

Sabina must've noticed my curiosity buzzing like a fly, "Only I and those I directly oversee are allowed in the manor during the day. Its daily maintenance is overseen by only me."

She wasn't the lady of the house...but I couldn't call her a housekeeper either.

I swallowed heavily. That peek through the curtain branded into my memory.

Sabina kept us out.

Sabina kept...something in.

She was the Warden and the dark feeling oozing from this place...

It felt like prison.

Chapter Twelve
The Lady of the Manor

Sabina did not welcome me into the fold; which was normal, apparently.

She welcomed no one.

We were simply needed for ground maintenance, and that was the extent.

She led us to a separate building, which was far more modern than the mansion and smaller. Where we will stay for the season. Mr. Martinez called it la Casita while Chuck, under his breath, derided it as an Outhouse for 'The Help'. Ricky elbowed him for that, but Mr. Martinez nor the Housekeeper corrected him.

To be honest, the building, with a full kitchen and two rooms, was a far more comforting than the opulent prison just on the other side of these gardens. A greenhouse with floral brocade black-iron bars framing the glass panels stood in the center between our new home and that prison masquerading as a mansion. Not only that, but this place, would definitely be a lot warmer than sleeping in a tent or in an old giant house that definitely was haunted.

Sabina stood at the doorway while we got settled in, dark eyes almost under long, bleached grey strands of hair; her presence was really hard to ignore. Maybe the casita was haunted as well; the temperature dropped several degrees whenever she stepped into a room. "Most of you know whereabouts the maintenance is needed most. Martinez, you will also look at the overgrowth near the lake."

It wasn't a request, but Mr. Martinez nodded. "Of course, Senora."

She glanced in my direction, and I shuddered. Her eyes narrowed, and I glanced down at my stomach. If I could rip open my belly button and crawl inside of myself at that moment, I would. It would be so much better than having black holes sucking what little of my crappy existence that I had left.

"I will come by 7:00 pm to escort you all for dinner." She never outright insulted us, but in the huff of her voice, it definitely felt like we were toddlers and she was the babysitter. "I rather have your meals sent here, but the Lady insists on having you for dinner."

The mood in the room suddenly lifted as I heard a quiet "Yes!" from Ricky. I glanced up at him and he had a nearly dopey grin on his face, a far cry from earlier.

With his words from before, I thought there was nothing good about this contract.

"We are looking forward to it!" The smile returned to Mr. Martinez's voice.

Sabina didn't even glance at him before turning her back. "After dinner, you are free to roam the mansion and the grounds. Just be outside or in here before the sun rises."

She was talking to me in particular. Chucky snorted, and Mr. Martinez merely coughed into his palm. Questions I had about 'the Lady' died from the silent laughter.

God, the floor was interesting, though were my laces always tied up like shit?

I can't even tie my shoes properly.

Was that hole in the sole always there?

God, why can't I disappear?

SHORTLY AFTER SABINA left us to our devices, we got back to the trucks. Mr. Martinez took the wheel while the rest of us younger guys were in the back with some chainsaws and weed eaters. We caught glimpses of dead limbs and neglected hedges on this impromptu tour, and I noted that the gardens around the mansion were green, yet oddly bare. Most of the flowers were perennials or still budded.

It was very weird...and honestly kinda creepy.

Back at my parent's the sun lit up the yard, making flowers bloom and arch towards the light. The trees danced and under my mother's green thumb, life flourished.

Here, everything hid in shadows. Shirking away from the light.

"Vampire plants." Ricky called then, motioning to the almost barren hedges around a rock and bamboo fountain, "Don't bloom except in the moon. Weird."

Mr. Martinez nodded, getting out a wheelbarrow sifter filled with fertilizer, "Floras de Vampiro. Only come out at night and drink blood. Carnivorous."

"You're shitting me." A guffaw was caught in my throat.

"Of course." He grinned, his usual jovial mood not tainted by Sabina. "But Junior is right. Only night flowers here."

The fertilizer set and the larger of the dead limbs removed, the sun was nearly set. Reds, purples and oranges flooded the courtyard and a trail of lights sprouted. I wiped my brow of sweat while the Ricky and Chuck fell onto the couch in the living room and Mr. Martinez rummaged the fridge for beer.

With all of them distracted and me smelling like shit (figuratively, thankfully), I called dibs on the shower first. I was the new guy and already I was on the client's shitlist; a shower was the least I can do to gain some favor.

If not with the housekeeper, then at least with the so-called lady.

Who was the lady? Besides the owner of this ridiculously large estate. If Sabina was exacting and cold, the idea of meeting the owner of the place caused my stomach to chew on itself again. I swallowed, heaving, fighting nausea as I finished buttoning up my flannel and sat down on the couch, my arms curled against my stomach.

"You okay, man?" Mr. Martinez patted my shoulder as Chuck shoved Ricky out of the way of the free bathroom, Spanish curse words fading into the background.

I shrugged; if I opened my mouth to laugh or answer, I'm pretty sure my intestines and shit would fall right out of my mouth.

Mr. Martinez gave a nod and glanced at his pre-dinner beer. "This job, it's not bad. It's good really. Senora can be uptight, but the owner; she's really sweet. Private but sweet. Good pay per the contract, lodging, food." He gave my shoulder one more pat and took a gulp of his Modelo. "Place is kinda spooky, but it's not bad for the season."

I nodded, my brow relaxing as I took another deep swallow, finally feeling my innards settle into place. "The owner...what's her name?"

Mr. Martinez paused in his drinking, pulling the bottle back and punching his chest. "Dunno." He confessed with a burp. "Since Sabina and Kenny are our primary contacts, we never got her name."

"The fuck? You three had dinner with her."

"The four of us did, you know, before he quit." He tilted his head towards the ceiling. "She never talked about herself. Mostly asked about us. Sometimes she was away, doing...what rich women do." His shoulders lifted, hands flexed out, "I dunno. All that matters is that she is nice and Sabina, while chilly, is respectful. Mostly."

I nodded, my fingers scratching arm through my sleeves. I was never absentminded about it; a part of my conscious was keen on peeling off my skin or adding some new scars to the fried collection. Bad habit; Zoloft helps.

The conversation drifted to some other things, maybe about beer. This was crappy for me to do, but I was barely in the casita. I was floating someone black and empty. I wanted to hide there as I waited for the grim reaper with platinum silver hair to appear and lead us on some doomed pilgrimage.

I am really poetic when I feel like the rotten juices leaking out of tipped over garbage cans.

A quick punch to the shoulder brought me back and when I looked up from the sofa, the guys were all washed, dried, and smelling like shared body wash. Specifically, my body-wash.

Assholes.

"Time to eat, sleeping beauty." Ricky motioned over to the open door. When I leaned forward, I could see the pale death glow of Sabina, her back to us as she waited, arms crossed.

I nodded, standing with shoulders slumped as I walked to the door.

I did not want to go to that manor, but my stomach, done eating itself, was dissatisfied.

Chapter Thirteen
Dinner Reunion

E veryone claims that the world changes at night.
Here, in this strange place, that was an understatement.

I have entered a new world.

Light hung from the trees, the forest boundary glowing with playful pastels that illuminated the leaves more so than the sun ever attempted. It was as if the stars in the sky floated downward to join the fireflies in a dance. Flowers that hid in dark green grasses blossomed in the moonlight and the fountain in center came alive, water triumphantly surging upward, sparkling in the night.

The life that hid in the daytime came out to greet us with a festival. If I wasn't being tugged along by the crew, I would've been too enraptured to move.

This could not be the same place.

The vines and foliage that hid away the mosaic tiles along the mansion walls now enhanced them; flowers of blue, red, and pinks opened open and their scent wafted to my nostrils. The smell was familiar. I stopped to stare up at that window, seeing it opened and curtains waving in the breeze. Sconces caused the fabrics to shimmer; what was once a prison became a retreat.

"Cole, stop perving, bro." Ricky's voice pried me away from the enchanting opened window and made my cheeks burned like lava.

I wondered if there was a hole I can bury myself in. I was a pervert; imagining how the room looked like, how big or small the bed would be.

Who I would share it with.

Warm, dark eyes that glittered like stars entered my mind. Eyes with rings like the center of trees, reflecting the wisdom of the ancients, while plum shimmering lips lifted in a coy smile. The void that awakened with Ricky's verbal jab retreated as I kept her and that night we spent together centered.

I was alive. I was doing something with my life.

Just so I can see her again.

With the moon illuminating the night, I kept in step with the rest, walking up the steps and into the opened double doors of the manor. Warm tones welcomed us in, and the interior of the manor was just as colorful and lush as the gardens.

We walked into wooden floors covered by long and plush Persian or Arabic rugs. Tufted chaise lounges and sections surrounding a lounge round coffee table were just off center of the foyer while an archway adorned with flower engraved wood displayed entrance to a parlor. Two staircases flanked the sitting area and a central round loft served as a patio room for another set of opened double doors. Mr. Martinez, walking alongside Sabina, whistled, verbalizing the awe I was feeling.

The manor was filled with the warmth of a large home and when I turned behind me, I could see a hearth crackling in the parlor. Much like the exterior in the darkness of night, this interior was nothing like I had expected. It was filled with color, and while definitely much more luxurious than I ever deserved to witness, there was something homely here. This must've been the work of the real owner of the estate.

It certainly was not the word of the noir specter besides my jovial boss. She paused before the second double doors, peering into the room. Curiosity made me lean somewhat to the side as she spent several moments with her head in the door, the straw strands of hair fluttering with the movement of her head. Ending her whispered conversation with an audible sigh, she pulled her head back and pushed the doors open.

Or did she push them?

Both her hands moved, but she did not place them on the doors. She waved at them and the doors just opened.

"The Lady is so rich she needs automatic doors, huh?" Ricky elbowed my sides, jutting his chin to the door.

Automatic, huh?

This Manor, with its fantastical colors, stone and wood architecture, seemed too old to have something so modern and practical.

Yet it had to be it.

Automatic doors that swung open slowly, no slight whir or buzz to be heard.

Okay.

Another elbow nudge and I followed Sabina and the crew through the double doors and into the dining room.

The honey glow of the pendant lights hanging from the arched ceiling enhanced the warmth of the long, mosaic inlaid wood table. Spices from the large ceramic serving platter filled my nostrils and my stomach growled at the sight of stewed meat and vegetables on top of a dome of tiny rice. No, it's not rice. Couscous, I think. I'm an idiot. I don't know what it was, but I know it looked delicious.

The black abyss that feasted on joy and happiness, leaving only dark, oily puddles of sadness, was nothing compared to the wanton appetite in my empty stomach. There bowls of various dips flanked each side of the large center platter and between each bowl were toasted flatbreads. Three chairs were at the side of the table. I gulped and shuffled towards one side of the table, following my two coworkers with Mr. Martinez staying behind to bring up the rear. I gripped the back of my chair, pulling it back.

"Senorita, you didn't have to wait for us!" Mr. Martinez's deep laugh almost made me jump. My eyes were so focused on the food, the floor, or the ceiling that I didn't even notice.

God, I must've looked a giant asshole. I cringed and just wanted to fall through the chair, through the floor and into hell itself.

"You know I don't mind waiting! Besides, I heard you hired someone new."

I froze, my hands gripping the chair as that voice broke through my embarrassment. My shoulders shook and when I lifted my head to face the head of the table, my jaw went slack.

Dark eyes that sparkled like a starlit sky looked back into mine. Dark, thick locks curled along her chin, puckered lips curled into a slight smile as she tilted her head and looked at me.

Mr. Martinez patted my back, but instead of the usual firm slap, it was full and thudded. I couldn't hear what he was saying. I think he was introducing me, but no introduction was needed.

Her name had been echoing in my head ever since that night. A prayer in my ears. That night, with her in my arms, her lips against my skin, came back and the beauty of this place at night made sense.

"M-Mallena..." Her name tasted like honey.

Yet the look in her eyes, her arched eyebrow and slightly uncomfortable chuckle, turned syrup into vinegar. "I'm surprised you know my name! I usually like to keep it a secret when a new person comes here."

What?

That didn't make sense!

"Mallena, what are you talking about—" I froze, the hair on the back of my neck sticking up straight, an electric shock causing me to tense further.

Abyssal ebony eyes stared at my own, light grey skin hands firmly tugging at Mallena's blouse, "My lady, dinner is getting cold." Sabina's voice come out low in a hiss and with that Mallena retreated to her seat.

Eyes were on me. Mr. Martinez's confusion, Ricky's embarrassment coming from under a palm on his face, and Chuck's own raised eyebrow took away my appetite.

Joy retreated. The colors danced and laughed.

I was the clown at the center, struck dumb and no longer able to eat.

Chapter Fourteen
Stolen Glances

I couldn't eat anything.

The food, which had smelled like heaven before, turned sour in my nostrils and my stomach churned at the idea of putting anything down my gullet.

I'm sure would disintegrate into mold and mush on my tongue.

So I sat there awkwardly like an idiot, my fork twirling the food around with the charm of an angsty teenager.

Or sullen toddler.

This would definitely be under one of my worst moments.

It didn't help that Kenneth and the chef (a really nice guy from Manchester) sat across from us. I'm sure I offended the chef by not eating, but thankfully, Mr. Martinez's ribbing and boisterous laughter distracted everyone.

Of course, his laughter could not stop creeping glare of Sabina, who chilly presence watched every single movement. What was worse is that I didn't WANT her eyes on me.

The person who I wanted to gaze at me, who I wanted to acknowledge me...pretended that I never existed.

Of course she did. Why would she want to remember your fucked up face? Or did you think you had a stunning personality?

You were a pity fuck. Nothing more.

She was probably even faking it.

All of those thoughts wrapped around me like tentacles, sucking away all of my progress and injecting me with skin-melting poison.

I was rotting shit and all other things that did not belong here. Not in this magical place.

The beautiful woman who I had worked so hard for the possibility of meeting again forget about me and there were a million reasons running through my head of why I was so fucking forgettable.

Honestly, the less I think about that dinner, the better.

My meds were not enough for this.

"Whoa! Cole! Bro, watch it!" Ricky slammed his gloved hands on my forearm, leading me away from the bright green thorns with close budded roses. "These are alive. Stick to the dead ones."

I turned off the motor of the handsaw, grimacing as I looked at his hand over my scars.

Ricky seemed to follow my eyes and pulled his hand back, curling it into a fist and bumping it against my shoulder. "Go help Chuck with the trees. Got a lot of dead limbs to cut."

I nodded, not really feeling like talking. Less black mud and bile falls from my mouth, puking out my rotting insides. I hated how he pointedly avoided looking at my scars. It had been so hot today that I had to roll up my sleeves. I didn't enjoy looking at my ugly ass skin either.

At least I didn't spend the past few days using shears to tattoo myself in blood. Instead, right after dinner, while everyone else wanted to catch up, I retreated like a bitch to the small guest house, curling up on the couch and using beer to dull the pain. The beer was, unfortunately, cheap piss water, so I had to contend with further wishing I was dead. I pretended to be asleep when the guys came back, and the following morning, everyone avoided asking me what the fuck was going on in my fucked up head.

Honestly, they probably saw this as another one of my episodes.

Which made me feel worse.

Apparently, from what I hear from Mr. Martinez, Mallena didn't join them for dinner. He only mentioned it to me, hoping to coax me back. I couldn't go back in there. Not yet. Not during the night where I would just drain the beauty of this place like the sun did. Chuck let me sulk, while Ricky stayed all business, though I knew he was irritated. Which is fair.

As much as he was annoyed, Mallena ignored me, and Sabina despised me. I was my own worst heckler.

I handed Ricky the saw before walking to the truck, missing the growling of the motor and how it overpowered the hissing whispers of loathing in my ears. The truck sat by itself in the unpaved lot, surrounded by nothing but the trees and overgrown gross, being stalked by the large gothic gate. It was weird; the manor was well kept on the inside, but besides Sabina and the big Mike Myers, Santa Claus, like Kenneth, no one else was around.

The truck, like the crew like me, was isolated.

I placed my palm on the edge of the truck bed, my head turning towards the dead Manor.

The sun was high in the sky, splotches of my skin getting into a pink tint. Yet the day when life retreated from the courtyard, the fountain, and the gardens. Even the stone and wood of the Mansion dulled, turning as grey and gloomy as the dreaded housekeeper.

And myself, to be honest.

Yet when I glanced towards that balcony, the glass mosaic, I can feel it. The hair standing on the back of my neck, the goosebumps along my arm. Even though I smelled rank of dirt mixed with sweat with the sun turning the pinks of my skin into some kind of mottled red, there was chill when I looked at that balcony.

A chill I only felt at day.

During the night, the curtains of shimmering silk billowed in the breeze. The golden light of the room enticed and comforted all who looked at it. The colorful mosaic shimmered like butterfly wings and blooming flowers welcomed all. Everyone who arrived here was a friend.

That only lasted until the sunrise, and then everything curled up into gray. The window would be shut, and the color retreated from the mosaic and the tower itself. The blooming flowers would shrink and the fairy tales that danced among the leaves would dim and die as the red oppressive rays of the sun rose higher and higher.

As bizarre as that was, the chill I felt was not from that devolution, but from the presence that was up there. It hid behind the curtains, in the dark corners that I could not see without climbing up to that window...or getting inside the mansion.

I wanted to ask the guys if they ever felt that presence, but much like the manor, even the jovial Mr. Martinez became more withdrawn during the day.

I'm sure I didn't make it any easier. Me and my emotional issues.

I'm a piece of shit who can't even get over a one-night stand.

All of that effort. That therapy, the stomach turning meds. All of that was for nothing.

What did I expect?

I blinked and shivered, rubbing my arms and feeling goosebumps. My eyes focused on the tower and I can feel that presence again.

Hiding, yet watching.

Staring at me.

I scratched idly as my upper arm, releasing the truck bed and walking back towards that manor. Beyond Mallena avoiding dinner (and myself), the presence hiding inside, the mystery that banned everyone else from entering this paradoxical place (I'm not that smart, I don't even know what that means), coaxed me forward.

Who was in there?

Was it Mallena? The woman who forgot I existed? Was she the presence I kept feeling? Was it her starry night eyes that caused my shivers?

Maybe the foreboding and eerie presence was her, silently cursing me away.

I moved towards the side, avoiding the front entrance in case the housekeeper/warden was waiting for me to fuck up. Going towards the side and then stepping into the back courtyard, I gazed up towards the balcony, backing up and then turning my head to see if there were any other entrances.

I could see the large back sunroom. The iron filigree bars lining large window panes brought to mind that intimidating gothic gate. I chewed on my bottom lip. Honestly, I wanted to bite it off at this point.

This was so stupid.

I need to get back to work.

Yet even though that sunroom was practically gated, the curtains over the glass panes were thick, blocking any light from slithering in, as well as keeping any wandering eyes from peeking inside.

Every single window I can see in this large manor was covered in curtains. I stepped further into the garden, walking along the edge of the manor where wooden boards, wrapped with chains, caught my eyes.

There was a broken window on the bottom floor, underneath an archway beside the house. The arch was covered in black, thorny vines, buds were roses would be. God, the back of my neck was itching now, seeing that board up window next to a chained up door.

Mallena, even during that horribly awkward dinner, was so lively. The night on the roof, she smiled, unashamed with joy. Her eyes sparkled in the nighttime and I'm positive that her skin with shimmer like gold in the morning sun.

So why was everything locked up?

Why were there no other cars for any crew to come maintain this place besides Mr. Martinez? Not only that, but Chuck and Ricky never seemed to question the oddities of this place and expected me, the new guy, to know the law here.

I was on thin ice already, yet the questions were forcing away my loathing and doubt.

Most of all, despite knowing that she found me so pathetic and forgettable, I wanted to see Mallena again. Just to say hello or thank her for at least pretending to give a shit about me.

As I starred at the boards, my fingers touching them, there was an obsessive urge to peel them off and see what the interior, that was so inviting during the night, looked like during the dreary day.

An urge that died as soon as a giant paw slammed on my shoulder, fingers digging in as I was spun around and was face to face with the angriest Santa Claus I have ever seen.

I was not on the naughty list.

Pretty sure I was on Kenneth's shit list.

"Holton, I know you know the rules! Why the hell are you sneaking around here?!" His voice was a deep bellow and if I wasn't so used to cussing drill instructors, I'm pretty sure I would've pissed my pants.

I tensed up, glancing up at him, my lips pressed tightly together. There wasn't a single excuse I could say.

Curiosity was selfish, and I was a piece of shit.

His brow furrowed, thick furry eyebrows narrowing into a single line. He definitely had the Mike Myers cross with Santa Claus look down. "You know, I've had enough of your shit. Where is your boss? I need him to drive your ass out of here."

He grabbed my shirt and tugged me away from the boarded window, letting go of me only to grab his walkie talkie. "Martinez? Or Ricky, one of you, your new guy needs to—"

The walkie talkie was no longer in his hands.

I didn't even blink.

I'm sure he didn't either.

One moment he was holding it.

The next it was in the gray-skinned hands of Sabina. Her nails dug into the plastic and those empty black eyes narrowed first at the struck silent Kenneth, then at me.

Her head jerked towards her shoulder, then straightened. It was a robotic motion that lasted a millisecond, and it made my stomach turn further into itself. I opened my mouth to make an apology.

Except I didn't.

I had no intention of apologizing.

"I need to speak to her."

White lashed fluttered over black eyes and her brow knotted.

I steeled myself. "I need to see Mallena and talk to her."

With Kenneth glaring at me in the background, towering over like a shadow, Sabina glanced at the walkie talkie, then back at me. "Fine. She will meet with you tonight, after dinner." Her voice lowered to a chilling hiss. "Now get back to work."

Chapter Fifteen
Moonlight Dalliance

I was certain that Sabina absolutely despised me.

If it was up to her and my serotonin drained brain, I would be a carcass at the bottom of the estate's lake, bloated or nothing but a scrap of meat on bones. She would've happily pushed me from the nearby cliffs and watched my entire body shatter as it hurt the ice cold water.

Luckily, she wasn't in the murdering mood.

Yet.

I followed her from the guesthouse to the forest. Trees loomed over us, the dim light from the crescent cascading through the leaves. Once again, I avoided dinner. If I ate anything, I would've puked it out from nervousness. When Sabina knocked on the door, I was in the middle of dry heaving into the toilet. My throat was scratched raw from the hoarse coughs and I'm sure my complexion was as gray and pale as the ghostly guide waiting for me.

She didn't even look at me as we walked further into the forest. There was a path before our feet, I could still see the dancing fairy lights above us, but the distance from everyone else at the manor made me...nervous.

Before I wondered how she was going to kill me and where did she plan to leave my body, the foliaged opened up. My jaw went slack as I gawked paths of blooming tropical flowers growing besides us. They wove and wound towards a glasshouse; gold plated iron vines coiled against the blue glass and the flowers loving embraced the doorway, aching for entrance.

We were in the temperate mountains! At night! How could tropical flowers blossom so verdantly?! My mother would go insane seeing this.

I already wondered if I was going crazy myself. I couldn't ask for a more beautiful grave sight.

Sabina stopped in front of the crystalline entrance, her hand hovering over the knob.

She was hesitating.

She turned her head sharply towards me. For a second her sclera went pure black and my heart clenched. Her eyes were bottomless holes and when they narrowed, I felt claws crawling up against the back of my neck, digging into the skin and injecting nitrogen.

I must've been imaging things.

I swear that second lasted hours.

Just her bottomless gaze, her empty eyesockets sucking out my blood and leaving ice instead.

Then it stopped.

The whites of her eyes returned and she sniffed, looking away from it.

The claws gripping the back of my neck released and I took heaving breaths, my arms wrapping around my torso, hands rubbing furiously to bring up the warmth.

What the fuck was that?!

My teeth shuddered as she finally opened the door, her head twitching towards it, "She's waiting."

I gulped, my lips numb. It took a few more rapid strokes to finally stop the numbing sensation. Hypothermia finally seem to fade away and everything was normal.

As normal as this place can get.

I couldn't even glance at Sabina as I walked inside of the glasshouse. I didn't want to see her eyeballs vanish, nothing but pure blackness sucking life inside. She embodied the void that mocked me and feasted on any type of emotion I felt.

I was terrified of her.

However, Mallena was waiting for me and for once in my shitty waste of a life I was going to man up and talk to her.

I needed answers only she could give.

The inside of the glasshouse was even more breathtaking than the outside. Strands of LED lights illuminated the floor and wrapped around the gold plated pillars holding the structure up. It was night and the fairy lights outside were dim, so I didn't appreciate the fact that each crystal pane was a different color. It was a rosette stain glass that reflected rainbow dance of joy within.

Everything was so stunning. The flora bloomed, and the scent wasn't overpowering at all. It was inviting and sensual, and the image of a skull with the abyss within was easily decimated.

I turned my head towards the door. It was closed and Sabina was nowhere to be seen.

How did I not hear her?

Nevermind, I didn't want to think about that ghost wearing gray skin and straw like hair. Not when I heard the familiar humming flowing in the air. My feet followed the sound, walking past playful topiary sculptures of butterflies, kittens, rabbits, and foxes. The fur and wings were made of brushes and perennials, and the scenes portrayed were that of welcoming spring.

In the center was an arch, lavished with more lilies mixed with roses. Under that arch was a gliding chair, swaying back and forth under the weight of the woman I stayed alive for.

Jesus that was pathetic.

But true.

She was just as stunning as that night she saved me. Dark hair cascading in thick waves down her shoulders, her light tan skin shimmered gold under the stained glass. Her head was tilted upward, her lips a small pout with the edges just lifted.

I froze, next to a flower and leave sculpted scene of cherubs, dancing along with foxes, bear cubs, and fawns. I wanted to hide. Already my nerves were getting the best of me. The disastrous dinner a few nights again held me firmly in place.

Even though I wanted to kiss those lips, to fall onto her embrace, I was terrified.

What would she say?

The moment I have forced myself to stay alive for was here. I could pretend that it was so I can see my family, so I can look in the mirror without seeing a shitworm starring back, but those were all lies.

All I wanted was to see her again and that moment was here and I am just being such chickenshit.

She was better off without me.

I was just wasting her time. Wasting her air.

I didn't deserve to be here, with her.

"Cole. It's rude to keep a lady waiting."

I swallowed the died mucus glob in more throat, my hesitation having led me to her grasp. I sidestep out of the shadows, my eyes downcast before I finally found my balls and stepped forward, "Mallena."

She tilted her head to the side, the corners of her mouth, tinted a cherry red, lifting higher, "I know it's been a while, but you don't need to be so shy."

I winced, the area between my eyes knotting painfully tight, "So you do remember me."

She grimaced, her smile faltering before she regained her composure and scooted over, patting an empty spot next to her, "Come on. Look at the sky with me." She giggled, her shoulders hunching, "It's quite a view."

Despite the hurt that shattered my sense of hope, the void gnawing at the back of my head, I couldn't resist her voice. I stepped closer, hoping the sleeves of my flannel kept my arms hidden. I sat down next to her and all of the tension left me. I fell limp and relaxed and the throbbing on the back of my head dulled.

This was right.

I looked up towards the ceiling, noting that the center of the rosette was crystal clear. I could see clusters of stars. They formed a tunnel, leading my eyes deeper towards space, towards galaxies far away. I sighed, wondering if this was what heaven was like.

I looked over to the woman next to me. The angel that saved me.

That ignored me.

I shuddered, leaning forward and resting my elbows on my knees. I couldn't just ignore it, could I?

The thick black fog had it claws deep in me and I made a mental note to up my dosage before bracing myself, "Why did you pretend to not know me?"

She sighed mournfully, still facing the stars, "It was the only thing I could think of doing."

"I know that it's weird to employ a one night stand, but..." It was so hard to figure out how the right words to use. Words that didn't make me sound so clingy, "You treated me like a stranger...I mean. One night stands are strangers but...fuck...you know..."

Her brow furrowed while her lips still held that sad smile, "It was more than a one night stand for me, Cole."

"Was it?" I finally got the nerve to look at her.

She nodded, her hands on her lap, fingers curling ontop of one another, "I meant every word in that letter. I enjoyed spending the night with you."

I couldn't stop the bitterness in my voice, "Was it just night of fun, then? Some good karma?"

Her smile vanished and her eyes narrowed, "Do you still think so little of yourself?"

Yes, of course I do.

I'm an stupid motherfucker but I wasn't going to answer that out loud, "What could I think? You vanished the next morning and when I finally see you again, you act like you didn't know me." My knee shakes and I can't bare to keep my eyes on her, "I have worked on myself, you know? Therapy, job...talking to my family again...I did all that because of you—" Stop it, dial it back, "—your letter."

I though I heard the slightest whimper as her knee pressed against mine, "Cole, I couldn't stay. I wanted to. I did, but I can't be in the sunlight." When I lifted my head, turning it to face her, her eyes were misty and glazed. Dark lashes fluttered over the rings of stars in her eyes, "When I found out that you were here, I was so happy."

She's lying. There is no way.

But I couldn't see the lie in those glassy eyes. I didn't see any deception in her gaze. Not in those barely parted lips. Those lips that closed tightly, pearly teeth chewing on the plump bottom half, "I was so happy, Cole. Happy and...and scared."

"Scared?"

She nodded, eyes closing and a tear falling, "You shouldn't be here. Why is god so cruel to me?" Another tear fell, her shoulders trembling and her chest heaving, "This is too cruel. I can't give you what you want."

What the hell is she on about? Why is she crying? She's rejecting me before I even ask the question...but she is in so much pain. How could someone like you suffer so much, Mallena?

My hands, riddled with tiny scars, lifted towards her tear-stained cheeks. I swallowed heavily, my nerves becoming as hard as steel, before pressing my palms against her cheeks.

My skin must feel like dried out and scratched up leather against her skin. Smooth like pearl and as soft as silk. My thumbs wiped away those tears, and when her eyelids opened, I thought I couldn't breathe. Much less speak.

I did my best though, "Mallena, what do you think I want?"

She sniffled, eyes downcast, "Something...normal. Something normal and healthy. I can't give you that Cole."

"Mallena, I don't want normal." Be brave. For once in your shit-stained life, be fucking brave, "I want you. The woman who almost fell a mile to the ground next to me...was never going to be 'normal.'"

"Cole, that's not what I meant—"

"I love you Mallena."

Fuck. They came out of my mouth before my brain could react. I wanted to bite off my tongue. I started to rip my hands away from her face, planning on dunking them into acid but when her palms fall onto the back of my calloused fingers, I froze.

Her lips trembled and she sniffled again, a gasping sob from her lips, "You love me? Cole, are you...are you serious? Do you m-mean it?"

Her eyes glowed and glittered with fairy lights. Her skin shimmered like gold and all of my fears, my doubts, vanished, "I loved you the moment we fell on the roof. The moment you held my hand and...and told me you wanted me to live."

She was crying even harder now, her fingers intertwining with mine, keeping my palms pressed against her cheeks, "I-I missed you. I wanted to see you again. I'm sorry I left you all alone."

God, she was worried about me. She thought about me. She wanted me to live and I did. I lived for this moment.

For her.

My lips pressed against hers and she kissed me back. I tasted salty tears, cherry gloss and chocolate from what must've been dessert. Her hands released mine to cup my cheeks and our lips pressed even tighter against each other. It was so hard to breathe in that kiss and I swear my lips were bruising from the intensity, but I did not and could not give a shit.

When she pulled back, air filled my lungs so quickly that I felt dizzy. She was panting, sniffling still and I leaned forward to kiss her again. She pulled back and my lips fell against her neck instead. I tasted sweat and the floral tang of perfume. Her fingers gripped my shoulders and then dug into my back, "Cole, I want you. I really do, but..."

I stopped, lifting my head as my blood went cold, "What is it?"

"The rules...you know? About the manor and day-day time." She gulped, one hand back on my cheek, her thumb rubbing my jaw, "We can't see each other during the day. Okay? I really don't do well...in the sunlight so you can't be in the manor after-after dawn."

The desperation in her eyes, the way her hand gripped the side of jaw firmly made it difficult to refuse what I thought was...unreasonable. Her eyes left no question and if being with her means becoming a night owl, so be it.

"I like my-my job Mallena...and more than that...I love you. Sure. I'll be with you only at night."

Chapter Sixteen
Nighttime Affairs

"I see that you and the lady are actually close, eh?"

I tried very hard not to choke on the meal while Mallena sipped her sparkling sangria; the deep reds coating her deep pink lips with a glossy plum. I could feel Mr. Martinez's eyes staring at the side of my head, along with a know-it-all grin hiding behind his mustache.

Chuck actually followed his nickname' sake, a low amused rumbled reaching my reddening ears.

"Come on, give Casanova some slack, dad." Ricky elbowed his dad, which only made Mr. Martinez guffaw. I could only give Ricky a half-hearted glare as he added to the tease.

So, maybe Mallena and I were not as discreet as I thought.

Only a millisecond after I promised to follow the bizarre 'Can't meet at Day' rule, we had devolved into an intense make-out session. My hands gripped her hips as her lips crashed against mine. We were practically devouring each other, both of us starving of the affection and passion we craved.

I still don't understand how such a deliriously sexy woman could be so desperate for me, but she was. When we fell down onto the grass in that cathedral like greenhouse, she had pulled up my shirt, her dress hitched up over her hips.

God, if we were only prepared with condoms that night. We had to separate from each other and I had to spray my blue balls with a hose before I could even think of walking into the guesthouse.

We did not make that mistake again.

The day after, I had to keep quiet. I was still suffering the effects of extreme embarrassment from the dinner of humiliation and while I stayed focus on the job, sawing down dead limbs and dragging them to the truck, it didn't help that the blue balls had turned to intense morning wood and I would not get caught jacking off.

So I worked as hard as I could. Trimming hedges, removing weeds, throwing fertilizer on grass seeds, rebuilding planter walls. You named it; I did it. I had spent the past few days moping like an idiot that I needed to make up to the guys...and distract myself from thoughts of what was to come later that night.

God, that was a sick joke. I am a terrible person.

Yet that night and every night since was...worth it.

It was always in the greenhouse and under the stars. Mallena would be there, waiting for me with that night's dessert. No, that was not a terrible joke, actual dessert...

Which 50% of the time would be completely abandoned once our lips met each other, our hands working off each other clothes.

Sometimes, it would be a slow tease; her hands peeling off my shirt inch by inch before she would coyly turn, moving her midnight black hair away from her back to reveal a zipper or even lace. She would force me to undress her slowly, which I would oblige by kissing ever open bit of skin. She would then taste my scars starting from my wrists, chest, even back. We slowly savored each other, silently at first, before our moans filled the air.

Other times, it was like the first night we shared; burning kisses, nearly torn off clothes, and embarrassingly animal-like grunts.

Well, for me it was embarrassing. Mallena...she was beautiful each time. Every sound she made was music, and I never wanted to stop holding her. Even when we weren't fucking on the ground, just talking to her on that naked immunity, made me feel...well shit.

I felt complete. Vitamin Z never made me feel like this. Being with her was effortless. Even if I was tired and exhausted from the day's work, I could come to her, make love, and then just spend the rest of the night with her.

Completely content.

The void was still there. That heavy fog that pulled on the back of my head and threatened to drag me down to the deep, reminding me I was a shit-bag. A shit-bag who stole some luck from someone else far more worthy and better than me. I was going to fuck it up, like I did everything else, and when I do, the void will be there to drown me in the filth that is myself.

Mallena deserved better than me. Even if she didn't believe it.

"Cole, I'm not getting naked with anyone else. Just you." She nuzzled under my chin and kissing my neck.

"I know. I feel like...this is a dream. When I wake up, you'll be gone and I'll wonder if you—"

Her fingers would press against my lips, and as I kissed them, a whisper reached my ears. "None of this is a dream. It's real. And we're happy. I'm happy." Those sparkly starry night eyes gazed into mine. "I want you to know that since spending every night with you...I feel whole."

Beautiful, confident, rich.

Why me?

I wanted to ask, but was too scared of the answer. Honestly, this would've one of those trick questions because no matter what answer she gave...it wouldn't be right.

Either it would make me feel like shit or I would think she was lying...and it would make me feel like shit.

So I never asked. I just...listened and kept holding her.

"Hey, Cabron, stop drooling over your girlfriend."

Ricky's voice cut through my memories and god I wanted to stab him. Okay no, not really, but it was getting frustratingly difficult waiting for dinner to end. Waiting for it to be just Mallena and me.

A songbird giggle filled the air. "I'm sure he's drooling over the Moussaka." She lifted a glass towards today's chef, grinning brightly. "Thank you so much, Tobias!"

Toby grinned back, "Well, these are my specialty's. I have some baked brie and baklava for dessert, so save some room!"

Chuck groaned, and Mr. Martinez laughed.

"I don't know how we're going to move tomorrow! We still need to work around the lake."

"You don't need to worry about the lake."

A chill sucked all the warmth from the room. Mallena's lips twitched and that effortless smile fade. Mr. Martinez blinked, color draining from his sun-baked face. "Senora?"

Sabina's eyes were on me, and she was sucking all life from the room, "I told Kenneth that the lake is going to become public property. The only thing you four will need to do is resize the boundary fence. Then leave."

I couldn't say anything. My mouth was suddenly as dry as a desert.

It was Chuck who spoke next, a quiet grumble, "Martinez...that's different from the contract—"

The woman, whose skin held no life and whose pale straw hair hung limply against her sharp angled cheeks, "You will be paid the same amount. I am only changing the contract."

That means that...I'd be leaving earlier...I wasn't even thinking about how...temporary this all is and now...we had less time than before.

"But-but you can visit anytime, of course. The gardens are so big, I would like some regular maintenance." Mallena's voice cut in, a higher pitch than usual.

Sabina's right eye twitched before both black pools of emptiness narrowed. She glared over at Mallena, and I was shivering. "There is no need for more regular maintenance. As head housekeeper and one who deals with the day to day running of this property, I assure you the gardens do fine with annual intensive care."

Plum glossed tips trembled and Mallena's eyes narrowed. "As-as I am the ow-owner of this property, I insist my gardens need-need regular attention." Her eyes darted towards me for a second before going back to Sabina.

"That is an unnecessary cost. Especially when we are cutting down the property line." Grey lips with a tint of blue pressed against a cup of water. I think I finally saw some life come to the ghostly woman's complexion, but she remained as cold as ever, staring down her own boss.

I wondered...who ran this place? Mallena was the homeowner, but now Sabina ruled with an ice cold grip.

"This...this is my home! I have a say in what-what needs help!"

"We need no more 'help' as necessary."

"That's not-not for you to decide, Sabina! None of this is for you to decide!"

This was getting personal.

Mr. Martinez stood up, nudging Ricky. "Er d-dinner was delicious, Toby. Bien provecho, but since we have to plan out the new property line, so we will get some rest."

Chuck nudged my arm, but I didn't make a move. Not when I could see the pain in Mallena's eyes.

I didn't want to leave. I didn't want to leave her.

"Cole, come on, let's go." Ricky whispered. However, his voice was not low enough.

"No! No, Cole doesn't have to leave!" Mallena's palms slammed the table, her brow knotted tightly, stars blurring into galaxies as her eyes misted over. "He doesn't have to leave if he doesn't want to!"

A low snarl escaped Sabina's lips. The emotion she held back and hid underneath a veneer of stark blankness erupted. "He is EXACTLY, who needs to LEAVE!"

I told you so...

I flinched, shoulders hunching as the fog descended.

I see.

Of course I should've seen.

This was my fault.

All. My. Fault.

Chapter Seventeen

A Happy Dream

"Don't blame him!"

My eyes widened as Mallena cried for me.

She cut through the fog, standing up and staring down Sabina like a lone, burning star in the night sky, "I want him to stay. You can't just sell off land to keep me alone!"

"I didn't sell it. I donated it. You don't need that much land and you don't need HIM!"

Chuck pulled me up from the chair as I stared blankly, like an idiot. I must've been weightless. He and Ricky pulled me up so easily.

What was happening?

How did this happen?

What did I do?

Exist.

That hissing void, spreading over my mind, dragging it down as I was dragged away from the dining room, my feet shuffling in a zombie gait.

You exist. That's why they are fighting. You exist and should leave.

Where?

Where would I go?

I planted my feet, shaking my arm free. Somehow, the guys and I were in the middle of the foyer and I looked back towards the dining hall, "Ma-Mallena."

"No, Cole!" Ricky marched in front of me. "You don't go in there. You know, maybe NOT fucking the mistress of the house should've been on the list of rules."

"Junior! Stop it!" Mr. Martinez didn't disagree outright, and honestly, Ricky was right. At least Mr. Martinez also didn't want to add to the chaos here. "Come on, let's talk more in the casita, okay? I hate the shouting."

Ricky glanced at his father before glaring at me, a finger jabbing at my chest. "Either your head is up your ass or you think with your dick!" He jabbed me again and I took it like a log.

I was not moving, though. Not now. My feet were roots, digging under the Persian carpet through the wood floors and sinking into the foundation.

The door opened and Ricky stomped off. I imagined that Chuck probably opened the main doors behind me because the only voice in the foyer was Mr. Martinez. "Cole. We need to go. This ain't our business."

Is he just as bat shit crazy as I am?

Of course, this is my business.

He and the guys...they were behind me now, fading away. My ears were on the shouting match; Tobias snuck away, hiding his head under his chef cap as he sauntered out from the room, leaving only the Star to screaming to the Black Hole.

"You do not know how I felt seeing him! I tried to pretend but I couldn't and now that I can be with him, I'm happy! Why can't you let me be happy?"

"This is a farce and you know it! All these years, all these disappointments and you still act like a child, Mallena! You know why he can't stay! You know why NO ONE can stay!"

"Sabina, he's different! He can be different!"

"Oh really? Because of his scars? Because of his self-esteem? I understand he is the most pathetic man you have brought home, but that doesn't change what will happen—"

Oof, she is really tearing into you.

Thanks for confirming what I already know.

You're welcome, shit-bag.

"He is NOT pathetic! He needs me!"

"He needs a therapist and YOU need to face reality! This will never work! You will only hurt each other! It will end the same way it always does and you know that, you stupid child!"

Silence.

Silence with a chill that flowed into the room. The doors shut behind me, leaving me to soak up the freezing air on my own. I swallowed heavily, still rooted to the floor like a sack of shit. I didn't know where to go and I didn't want to leave. Not when the night was so young.

Not without her.

Hurried steps left the dining hall and Mallena came into view, tears staining her golden cheeks. Her bottom lip quivered before she sniffed, forcing a smile. "You're here. You're still here." She wiped her eyes with the back of her wrist, "C-Come, let's go—"

"Mallena!" A bony ivory hand gripped her other wrist, attempting to pull her back, "You will only hurt him and he'll..." Abyssal black eyes glared at my direction, making my heart stop, "He'll disappoint you like the rest!"

"Enough!" She tore her wrist away from the wraith, running just past me. Her fingers intertwined with mine and the roots keeping my feet attached to the floor dispersed.

Even though I outweighed her, she pulled me with no effort. I was powerless as she went up the stairs instead of out the door.

"Mallena! Mallena, listen to me!" Sabina called after us from the bottom of the stairs, "Mallena, you are only going to hurt him! Please listen to me!"

Please?

That cold voice, stern with shards of ice, had melted into a desperate plea.

A plea for that Mallena, her hand tightly wrapped around mine. I watched her back, following her through hallways, through more stairs that spiraled upwards. Sabina's voice became a memory as the Lady of the Manor tugged me after her, leading me to...well wherever she wanted to go.

She finally paused in front of an open door, her fingers trembling in my large hand. We stood in front of that doorframe for seconds...minutes? I wasn't sure. The intricate rainbow glass and nickel hanging lanterns on each side of the door sparkled with colors, beckoning us to enter.

Yet she hesitated, shuddering as if in the center of a freezing storm.

I swallowed heavily, coming back into my body. "Ma-Mallena?"

Her shoulders hunched sharply before going lax. She didn't glance back at me, nor at the stairs behind us while she walked in, guiding me to her.

As I stood in the center of the room, still struck dumb, her hand released mine. The door behind us closed, while another remained opened.

It was the large double window, going from ceiling to the floor. It was a portal to the night sky; to the forests that sparkled with fair lights. To the flowers that bloomed only in the moon's light and under the glittering of the stairs.

Mallena stood in the center of the frame, gazing out to the world from the balcony.

This balcony.

This was her room along.

"...When I first...saw you." Her small fingers motioned behind her, beckoning me as she spoke. "Right under here. When you were staring at the little gems in the stone...I was scared."

Finally, I was back in my body, able to work my vocal chords without the fog dampening them, or Mallena overpowering every single sense I had. "Y-yeah...you said that before."

"Cole...I was terrified."

I blinked, my jaw going slack again. "Why?"

She didn't respond. At least not with words. She turned her head towards me, her eyes barely opened. They sparkled again, but with tears. Shining tears that glowed under the moon and traveled in thin blobs down her shimmering cheek.

Compelled, one of my calloused hands, littered with shrapnel divots, pressed against her cheek, one thumb wiping away those salt bubbles from just under her eyes, "Sabina?"

"She-She's right, you know? I c-can't make-make you happy. No-not like you de-deserve." She sniffled again, a sob choking out of her plump lips.

"M-Mallena, I am in-in therapy, you know? I've go-gotten help. Because of you."

Her head shook, long voluptuous locks falling against her face. My other hand pressed against her free cheek. As I cupped her face, she hiccupped, the tears still falling, pooling between my palms and her cheeks, "Cole, if you knew the truth. If you-you see me...you'd run. You would run f-far away. You would have to run."

"Are you crazy? Mallena, I will see you. I SEE you. You brought me so much joy. I have been seeing you since the top of that building. All I have been seeing is YOU." The words were falling out of my mouth and my god it was all true, "I missed you. I adore you. I love you. Because of YOU I am here and happy. Deliriously happy."

Her hands moved over mine, fingers circling my own. She gripped them, trying to move them from her face, "...I'm so selfish. I am so selfish. I wanted to hear those words for so-so long...but...but..."

"Mallena. These words are true. As long as I'm with you...I'm happy." That was true. The voice retreated with her. The fog dispersed when it was just us together.

I exist, because I am with her.

Her fingers laid flat and her eyes opened wider, gazing into my own, "C-Cole...I want you to-to stay. Will you stay with-with me?"

Damn straight, I want to stay. For a millisecond, the rule about daytime flicked across my head. Yet looking at those sparkling lights in her eyes, down at her lips, her plea ringing in my ears, I ignored it. Fuck the rules. She wanted me to stay.

I wanted to stay.

"Of course I will." My lips pressed against hers, just barely. "I will stay." I pulled back, only to kiss her again, and again. Each word punctuated by a kiss that grew longer and deeper than the last. "As long as you want."

Her lips parted against mine and I held her close, delving into the kiss as deep as I could go. Her fingers fall from my hands and onto the loops of my pants, pulling me against her. Again, I was enthralled; she pulled me back and back, until we fell on the bed, lips still attached, tongue deeply tasting each other. I shuddered, pulling back at her legs wrapped around my waist, my hands pulling up her skirt, hooking onto the sides of her underwear.

I slowly dragged them down, lowering myself down past her chin, neck, breasts. The satin fell to the floor and my lips pressed against her inner thighs, letting the smell of her fall on me like perfume.

"C-Cole...help me dream. Help me dream about us...make me happy."

How could I refuse?

When my lips pressed between her thighs, when her moans filled my ears, all I could think about was her happiness and how I will spend the rest of my life making her dreams come true.

Starting with tonight.

Chapter Eighteen
Nightmare Awakening

"Stay awake, Cole..."

I nuzzled against the most perfect breasts in existence. "I'm awake..."

"I mean, Cole. Stay—" Mallena paused for a second and then released a loud yawn that echoed throughout the room, "Stay awake..."

I couldn't stop my chuckle, raising an eyebrow as I looked up at her. "What about you?"

She lightly slapped my back, pouting with her perfect lips, before she leaned forward and kissed the top of my head. "This is my bed, my room...my MANSION." She flicked the tip of my nose before kissing it. "I'm only staying awake for moral support."

I nuzzled under her chin and against her neck, "I know I can't sleep here...but...one day...I'd like to wake up next to you."

She was so lax and fluid like satin that it was noticeable to feel her tense like a statue. Every muscle in her stiffened under me and I could feel the fog in the back of my head descend. I pulled up onto my palms, gazing down at her, "I mean, if-if you feel ready. Or-or we can keep just me-meeting at night." Those sparkly eyes grew hazy and glossy and I wished I could rip off my tongue. When a tear fell, I whimpered, pressing my hand against her cheek, "No, don't cry...not again—"

"Cole. I'm happy." She sniffled, kissing my palm. "I am thrilled. I've been so a lone all this time, waiting to hear someone say that they...love me."

"Mallena..." I kissed her forehead, then one cheek, before leaving a slightly wet kiss on the tip of her nose, "I will happily say that again and again." I gently guided her chin forward, kissing her lips, my mouth sucking on her bottom lip, making her coo against my skin. "I love you." My lips press against hers again. "I love you." Her quickening breaths, her hard nipples dragging along my chest, caused my lips to press hard, my hips to grind. "I love you." Her lips parted with a moan and my tongue delved into her open mouth, tasting all of her before I pulled back just barely, swallowing her breaths. "I love you."

Her eyes closed and her head leaned back as I gripped the sides of her thighs. She spread them for me and her squeal against my shoulder ignited a second wind. A condom was hastily pulled out of the drawer and once it was wrapped around my cock, nothing could stop us. One hand gripped my back as we rocked against each other, her wet mouth against my ear, "I love you too, Cole. I love you..."

Our words were a prayer to each other, our bodies coalescing into a single being. A single heart, a single emotion. It drove me forward, sweat, tears, cum and juices smearing against the sheets. We held each other, loving each other, and the fog faded away, leaving us in heavenly, perfect isolation.

"Stay awake...Cole..." She licked my cheek and neck, making me melt in the afterglow, "Stay awake..."

"I will...I'll...stay...awake..." For a second my eyes felt so heavy. Her ASMR whispers became a lullaby. I had to blink just once. Just enough to clear my head, recover a third wind and get off of this cloud soft bed.

Just one blink...

It was a nudge and then a drop of thick fabric over my head that snapped my eyes open. At least they would be opened if they were covered by the quilt. Hurried breaths coming from the side of me brought me further into the light—

Light?

I inched down the blanket, seeing a faint orange glow coming through the window.

Shit. Oh shit!

I did not stay awake.

I turned to my side, relief settling in seeing a familiar satin clad bottom in front of me, "Mallena—"

She jumped away from my touch and shoved a pillow in my face. "D-Don't look at me! Don't look!"

What the fuck? "Mallena, I know. I'll get out of here." I tossed the pillow to the floor before I huffed against the palm of my hand, sniffing it. My breath couldn't be that bad that she needed to be as far away as possible.

"No! No, you can stay. Just don't look at me. Please don't look!" Each word out of her mouth ended in a gasp. She was hyperventilating.

"Mallena?" I shoved the quilt off of me, pulling up my boxers while she hurriedly put on a long tunic shirt.

Her body was trembling, her head looking at the window before she ducked under my hands, running to the curtains, "Cole! Please keep your eyes closed!"

"Mallena, what...why are you so scared?"

The room glowed from the morning sun and she screamed, dashing away from the sunlight slithering from under the curtains. "Leave! Cole, please leave!" I wasn't even holding onto her, but she ran from me as if I was a ghost.

Why...did...I scare her?

No, it wasn't me.

Don't be an idiot!

Don't let the void talk.

What does she not want me to see?! When she grabbed my arms to pull me out of the door, I turned away, gripping her shoulders. "Mallena, why are you freaking out? Talk to me!"

Her bright dark eyes were wide and empty of anything but fear, tears down her cheeks. "Don't look at me! Please don't look at me!" She lunged forward, her palms pressing against my eyes. "PLEASE STOP LOOKING AT ME!"

The heat from the sun hit my neck and jaw, my hands moving up to peel her fingers away from my eyes. "Mallena! What is going on!?"

Her fingers fell from my eyes and...

Everything burst into flames.

There was no window.

There was no door.

I was not in the mansion anymore.

I was not in her bedroom.

Where ever it was, it was the last place I wanted to be.

My ears popped from whizzing metal pebbles, breaking through the crackling, snapping sound of flames devouring wood, stone and flesh. The smell of cooking meat filled with my nostrils and I heaved, bile and moussaka bubbling from my stomach, through my throat and onto the floor. I collapsed, hacking out the contents of my stomach, mucus and saliva before another bullet whizzed past my ears, forcing me to curl up on the ground.

There was so much black smoke. It stung my eyes and filled up my nose and tongue. I couldn't even smell or taste my vomit anymore; I could only taste smoke. The heat was sucking away moisture, and I crawled through the smoke and ash towards...I don't know where!

I had to get out of here! I had to get out of this hell!

Mallena. Where was Mallena?!

She was screaming too, right?! Was she still in this hell? Did she make it out? Where did she go?

I heaved, trying to get whatever air I could, even if it was smoldering black smoke tore at my lungs, ash cutting into my throat.

What if she didn't get out?

What if she was still in here?!

"Ma-Mallena..." There was no saliva left in my throat. I had no moisture left at all. I gripped on the only thing that wasn't crackling into and dragged myself up, coughing into my arm, "Ma-Mallena!"

"C—Cole..."

I looked up towards what — who I grabbed as I tried to blink away the smoke, "Malle-"

Sunken eye sockets oozing with red blood and liquid puss were looking back at me, skin peeling off from muscle then bone. Black cracks burst open with flowing crimson and there were no lips, not anymore. The plump skin was dripping off of its face like wax, exposing gums and teeth in a scream.

My god the scream.

A cacophony of voices, coming out of a blister covered throat hit my ears and my hands ripped away from ...this THING that I had held onto. My nails were coated in gelatin gore, which then slithered into my ears when I tried to plug them away from the SCREAM!

I thought I heard my name, but that all melted away into the gasping, garbling sound, smoke and burnt meat invading my burning nostrils. The words I could make out rippled through in English, Farsi, Arabic, all the languages I heard in my deployments. They branded my brain and fed into the void that latched onto chained itself around my brain, weighing me down into blackened rot and crude oil.

Coward!

Killer!

Failure!

Shitbag.

The void.

It was here.

In those eye sockets, now empty of fluid and flesh. It stared at me from the abyss, taunting me in every single language in the world, wearing the melting, searing body as a suit. I fell on my ass, the smell of ammonia and sulphuric meat, causing me to throw up again; acidic bile poured down my neck and chest as I desperately backed away from the burning, gore marionette shambling towards me, screaming as the void gloated.

I was a complete, worthless, sham.

I knew that. I always knew that. Yet never had my body felt so FULL of that truth. I puked out everything, leaving only that fact as I sobbed and crawled away. An opening out of the smoke and ash Hell came into view and I took it. I took it as fast as I could while snot and tears coated my face and joined my vomit covered chest and pissed coated thighs.

Once I was out of the room, I felt ice-cold fingers grip my shoulder, shoving into calloused arms. Those arms were dragging me down the stairs, a towel thrown over my shoulders as I pulled farther and farther from...hell?

I coughed, my throat raw as I glanced back towards the inferno, cooking rotting gore and screaming families.

Yet, through my stinging eyes, I could clearly see no smoke. No orange and yellow blaze. The screams were echoing in the back of my head and anguished sobs came from that room. Familiar, pained sobs.

"Ma-Mallena—"

"Shh, shhh Cole. Come on, kiddo, we have to leave."

The calloused, leathery hands belonged to Mr. Martinez. I tilted my head, gasping in air as I looked up at him.

His brow was knotted into tight and deep valleys, his lips set in an uncharacteristic frown. He shouldered my empty weight out of the foyer, past the manor doors. All the way, those cries filled the overbearingly opulent estate.

Footsteps, heavy and quick, were behind us and when we were outside, I could hear Sabina's voice. Normally cold as ice, it was frigid, seething with frostbitten rage. "You stay away! You stay the fuck away from here!"

I tried to turn my head, knots ripping from my muscles, but Mr. Martinez shook his head, pushing me into the backseat of the truck. Someone threw blankets over me and the truck door closed.

Yet I could still hear the housekeeper's voice frosting the windows.

"You are FIRED! The contract is void! YOU STAY THE FUCK OFF OUR LAND!"

I tried to claw my way up, to look out the window.

Where was Mallena?

I couldn't see her. All I could see was that balcony window, smoke billowing from it. "Wait-wait...Mallena—"

"Shut the fuck up, Cole!" Ricky was in the front seat. He must've tossed the blanket over me. Mr. Martinez silently got into the truck and we left.

He did not look at me once. Ricky didn't either.

Only the void, glaring from that melting, screaming face, or from the icy black glare of Sabina, remained.

I...

I am...a complete...shitbag.

Chapter Nineteen
Post-Traumatic-Stress-Disorder

"Cole, you okay?"

I hated hearing his voice. Despondent, careful. He's walking on eggshells.

Mr. Martinez wasn't the type to walk on eggshells.

Then again, he probably had little experience seeing someone lose their shit as spectacularly as I did.

Or maybe he did.

When I looked up at him, I saw the sadness.

The pity.

He probably seen a lot of guys like me breaking down from the stresses of civilian life. Shellshocked bastards, paranoid about every single sound outside of windows, every tick of the clock, every pop of a wheel hitting a pothole, suddenly snapping. Rampaging about being watched, hunkering down expecting the next strike, or just going mad, screaming and crying as they relived watching one of our brothers, sisters, or even a bystander, die in their arms.

That...isn't what happened to me. Yet how could I explain it? I could explain making love to a beautiful woman one moment and then being surrounded by fire and burning flesh the next? How could I explain searching for the woman I loved, only to find a screaming mass of melting bodies in her place?

I couldn't explain it and remembering it?

Fuck, I felt the tears fall from my eyes before I could stop it.

He grimaces, the frown on his face, the knot along his brow. He aged decades without his jokes, "Now, I won't ask what happened back there. Junior may have mentioned Danny...he was one of the crew. Before you, I mean. He broke down too. He was looking for something in the Lady's house and...ran out screaming. Scratching at his eyes. Chucky had to knock him out to get him to the truck." He rubbed the gray hairs on his chin as he leaned forward, elbows on his knees, "Couldn't get him to tell us what happened. Senora, she was pissed. Said this could never happen again." He rubbed one of his eyes before dragging his hand along the back of his neck, "I had planned the next season to be just us three, but you..."

He looked over at me again, but when his eyes met mine, I looked down, staring at the IV tube sticking out of the back of my hand.

I heard him shift in the chair. "You were working so hard. Each time I saw you at the group, you lightened up, you laughed, and talked about your mama and her gardens. You needed someone to give you a chance. And I wanted to give you that chance."

I closed my eyes, scratching at the IV needle burrowing under my skin.

Here it comes...

"Cole, I got the contract back, but Sabina made it...superbly clear that no one but Chucky, Junior, and me can be on the property. Kenny volunteered to help with the weed whacking, tree chopping, all the rest." His gruff scoff revealed his bitterness.

Kenneth was going to be watching them.

A prison guard watching over laborers for any transgressions.

I bit my bottom lip.

Mallena...

Sabina was her warden.

And I royally fucked everything up.

"So until this contract is up, you are on leave. Ah, paid, of course. Short-term disability. Until you get out of here," God, his laugh sounded so fucking forced. "Then...call me. Talk about what the job looks for you. Maybe start with you doing part time, okay?"

Stop wasting your pity on me. I don't deserve it. Just fire me.

I could only nod, letting my upper back and head fall onto the bed afterwards, the counting the number of beeps in the background.

Mr. Martinez coughed into a closed fit, and I heard the chair squeal as he stood up. "Well, I think the nurses are coming to check up on you, lady killer."

Liar. The nurses will not come for another 30 minutes.

"You take care, Cole. I'll see about having the other guys come. Get well soon."

I closed my eyes tightly as his footsteps faded until the door swung opened and then closed. When the sound of him vanished into the hall, I gasped. Then I cried.

I cried and scratched at my arms and eyelids until two nurses came in and held me down, an on call doctor sticking a sedative into my IV.

Which was...the worst.

Cause that means the nightmare would come back.

Why...?

Why didn't I listen?

"DON'T LOOK AT ME!"

I'm so sorry...Mr. Martinez...

Mallena...

Everyone...

I'm so sorry.

That's not enough, shit bag.
It will never be enough.

"HELLO RICARDO. YEAH, we got him home. He's resting and Gene is going to have his prescriptions delivered here..."

My mom's voice waded in and out of my ears. She sounded exhausted. The parasite came back and sucked out the air that should've gone to some other kid. Some kid who wasn't filled with worms and shit writhing in the back of their head. I laid on the bed in the room that belongs to a much better son. A son who died and was replaced with a fucked up shell. I didn't deserve parents like her. Like dad. Why did they waste their time picking me up?

"...Thank you. It's great of you to check up on him. I don't think he's ready to get back to work." When her voice came back, I could it crack, a sniffle pausing her side of the call, "...no I'm okay. Don't worry. I'm just happy that he had someone to help him..."

Help me, huh? After I nearly cost him a job. After I pissed myself and was a comatose sack of shit or a wrist-cutting manic idiot? Why did he even bother?

"...No, he hasn't talked about it. No, no, don't tell me and don't tell Gene. Cole will talk when he's ready."

A pathetic whimper escaped my lips, and I curled up on my side, closing my eyes so the flashes of cooking corpses and melting jelly from eye sockets could stop.

Are you going to tell her how you fucked the homeowner and then screamed like a bitch in the morning? Running with pants down like a scared little boy? You worthless piece of shit.

Stop...please just stop.

The void wouldn't stop.

Its black miasmic presence weighted down my head and shoulder, enveloping me and feeding me more bits and bobs of the phone call that I really didn't want to hear anymore.

"Yeah, yeah sure. I can keep you posted. Cole loves working in my garden, so I know he'll want to come back. I really appreciate it. You both deserve so much thanks for your service..."

My service?

The service I was medically discharged for? After continually waking my squad up with screams in the middle of the night after the bombing? After almost sending our convoy off the dunes because I couldn't sleep during the night?

They were happy to get rid of you. Deadweight.

The throbbing at the back of my head spread to my temples. I closed my eyes tightly, grimacing through the pain, my fingers digging into my sides. Each time I tried to shut the void out, the screaming skull with molten jelly gushing from black sockets comes back. The melted, roasting abomination of congealed bodies writhing in flames fills in the blanks where the void would be and I don't fucking know which one is worse!

I want to die.

Why did I even bother living?

Why did Malle—

I cough into my head, swallowing the vomit that almost launched out of my mouth.

I can't even say her name.

If it wasn't the phone call of despair and pity that sucked soul out of my parents or the smoke filled stone prison riddled with bullet holes and charred screaming carcasses, then it was the wailing that haunted me as I was driven away.

The grieving sobs of the woman who saved my life. Who asked me to make her happy?

I failed.

I fucking failed as a soldier, as a civilian, as soon...

As a man.

I pushed myself up from my side, staring out the window of the room that belonged to a little boy who grew up to be a piece of a shit. I saw my dad walk out of the car and my stomach fell further into Hell.

I couldn't stand another day seeing his disappointment.

Another day, hearing phone calls of pity.

Another day of my mom begging me to eat, sobbing as I ignore her. It had to stop.

The nightmares keeping me awake.

The void eating me alive.

The waste of money my parents and the government throw at therapy and medications.

I had to stop.

I had to stop...*existing*.

Somehow, when that thought entered my head, it was like the tiniest bit of light at the end of a very long tunnel. A light that flickered and pulses as the tunnel closed up like a sphincter before opening again. An escape out of a shit-filled tunnel as disgusting as I am.

If I had just killed myself back then, none of this would've happened.

"The view is wonderful, isn't it?"

I kicked my legs over the side of the bed, staring down at my feet.

If only I flung myself off the building.

"I think enjoying the evening is better with company, right?"

I pulled on the closest shirt I had before pulling on my pants.

I was dressed then. At least my corpse shouldn't be naked.

"So you can hog this glorious sight to all of yourself?"

I'm sorry mom, dad. I need to borrow your car, but don't worry, it'll be fine.

It's still worth more than I am.

"I don't want you to feel that way."

I want to die.

"Why?"

I have to die.

"I want to see you again."

I can't keep living like this. I can't be a burden.

"I want you to stay alive, Cole. Because that means that I can see you again."

I couldn't even stand to look at her. I wanted to wake up seeing her smile and holding her in my arms.

I couldn't even give that to Ma-Mallena...

"C-Cole...I want you to-to stay."

I love you.

"I love you too, Cole."

I want to see you again, before I go.

At least I need to make it up to you.

My parents are too busy talking to each other in hushed voices to notice me creep out the front door. They don't notice the keys missing from the hooks in front of the coat closet.

I close the door as quietly as I could and go to the car.

I need to go somewhere far away. Then I'll fill up the car, park it just out of some scenic viewpoint and then launch myself from the sky to the earth.

"Don't look at me! Please don't look at me!"

Mallena...

What the hell happened?

I get why I want to get the hell off this Earth, but you...why did you want to join me?

Why do you want to die too?

Chapter Twenty
The Truth

It's surprising what trauma forces you to remember.

The wooden crossing gate, the lake on the other side against the cliffs...

A muscular Santa Claus guy named Kenneth aiming a shotgun at my parents' car.

My hand gripped the steering wheel tightly, my jaw set so tight it felt like I had stitched my mouth shut.

I stared back at him; the headlights illuminating his face. He had stepped to the side, proving to me he was, in fact, a real human being holding a real shotgun.

I really didn't want to him to shoot my parent's car.

I already cost them so much already.

His lips curled down and to the side beneath his mustache and he motioned towards himself with two fingers. I gulped and pulled the car into park. Thank god it was night time because all I had on was jeans and a tank top.

Every single burn, every single ugly indent painted on my skin, was in view. I was covered in craters and when I stepped out of the car; I grimaced as the night breezed clawed into old wounds.

Kenneth's eyes narrowed, though I doubt he gave a shit about my fragile vanity, lowering the shotgun to the ground, "Mr. Martinez should've told you not to come here."

I nodded, "He did."

His frown pulled his lips downward, his brow furrowed. "Then why are you back here? Go home."

"I need to see her." My eyes downcast as I rubbed my arm. "I need to talk to her."

Kenneth aimed the shotgun at my face. "You have done enough. Leave!"

My lips pressed tightly together, the back of my head weighed down by the fog, "I need to know what-what happened. I need to know what happened to Mallena."

"You broke the rules." Under that beard, the whiskers rustling with each vibration. "Get back into your car and go home."

Go home and get into your bed. Hide from the world and dissolve into rot. That's all you are, parasitic rot, leeching off of parents since you drove away your friends.

I grit my teeth. Grinding the rows side by side was the void, and blackness crawled and spread from the back of my head forward. "I-I can't go back. I'm not planning ongoing back."

"God dammit, Cole! You left her a wreck! She hasn't shown her face to anyone! Not even Sabina!" His voice vibrated with his growl, but I could hear the sadness seeping through.

The pity.

Mallena must have grown tired of that, too. The pity that oozed out of everyone around her. The pity that she couldn't stave away with whimsical words and coy smiles.

"I didn't mean to and I-I didn't want to leave. What I saw...what she turned into...I can't describe it! I just want answers—"

"There are no answers! No one knows, and no one cares about you saw!" Kenneth cocked the shotgun, pointing straight at my head, "Now get back in the car and fuck off before I blow your goddamn head off."

That...wouldn't be a bad way to go. "Do it. Shoot me. Put me out of my fucking misery!" The words tumble out of my mouth like vomit. "I can't get it out of my head! First the fucking IEDs in the desert and now walking to a screaming mass of melting, roasting corpses! I can't stop seeing it!" My nails tear into my arms before I could even register the motion, "The room was in flames and I was choking and that...that thing was screaming! That thing that...that was Mallena!" I ripped off skin as I stomped closer to Kenneth.

Suicide by muscular, angry Santa Claus.

That will send me straight to the naughty list.

Kenneth could see the blood down my arm, his eyes focusing on the red that glowed from the headlights. He lowered the barrel just barely. "Look, I get that you're fucked in the head, but you ain't getting answers because I know nothing! All I know is that you ain't the first dumbass to go fucking nuts and you won't be the last! Now I mean, I will shoot—"

"THEN SHOOT ME!" I didn't know if I wanted answers or just that fucking ebony fog to lift its damp, cloying weight off my head and shoulders. I slouched forward, the barrel now against my chest, "Fucking shoot me! Either give me answers or just...just end it so I don't have to hear her cries anymore! Hear her sobbing. I know I fucked up, but the screams...her tears. I failed so many people and the last thing I wanted was to fail her..."

Goddammit.

I'm fucking crying.

This Paul Bunyan looking guy has a shotgun digging into my chest and I am slobbering drool and tears onto the metal, "I just want to know what happened...I just want to know so I can say I'm sorry. Sorry for failing her when she needed me the most. If I can't have that, then just shoot me."

I bit down on my bottom, trying to stifle my sobs. I didn't even feel the metal lower and move away from me. Sobbing like a wimp, I just stood there. Maybe he should just shoot me. I can't get any lower.

Instead, he shook his head, "Just...damn it. I don't even know what you did, Cole. The only one who knows is Sabina, and she doesn't want you near the poor girl anymore."

Though choking gasps, I nodded, using my scratched up forearms to wipe my tears. The salt dug into my scratches; the sting distracting my mind enough from the hole it was drowning in. "I didn't want to hurt her. I love her."

Kenneth grimaced. His lips must be pursed together somewhere under his beard. Look, I know I kept focusing on it, but it was the beard or adding another weight to my self-hatred. He sighed again; the whiskers flowing upwards before he held up a finger. His eyes shifted from me and towards one ear. He nodded, his brow relaxing just barely.

I could tell he was listening to the voice in his earpiece, most likely the one person who wished I was dead more than myself. He closed his eyes, his shoulders lifting and then lowering, "All right. I'm gonna take you to the greenhouse. Sabina will be there."

I sniffled, the void in my head mocking me as I do. "How is Mallena?"

Kenneth motioned with his head, the shotgun hanging against his thigh, "You can ask Sabina. She's the only one who knows what happened."

As I followed him to his truck, I realized Sabina was the only person who ever came in and out of the manor during the day.

If I couldn't talk to Mallena just yet...then at least I can find out the truth.

Whatever the hell the truth is.

Chapter Twenty-One
The Witch's Curse

Though I already knew that Mallena wasn't there, seeing only the gaunt figure of the icy housekeeper did not stop the disappointment. Kenneth stood just off to the side, between me and Sabina.

At least, I thought it was her.

We stood there in silence and I swear every other time I blinked, the woman before me changed. For a split second, her skin would be bone-white leather with deep valleys cutting down the sides of her mouth and underneath her eyes. Her body, already slouched, would slump forward and those abyssal eyes seemed to sink further into her sockets, devoid of light and life.

Yet at the nice blink, Sabina would appear as she normally did. Much like the tropical flowers that bloomed where they shouldn't, there was something about her that made little sense.

Honestly, between the manor, Mallena, and Sabina, I could one hundred percent concur that absolutely nothing here made sense.

Yet.

Again she aged centuries, her breaths shallow and her fingers thin as claws. When she lifted her head, I could hear the pops of her joints. Yet once she looked at me, the wrinkles were gone and life, unforgiving life, came back to her gaze. "Kenneth, go back to work."

Kenneth's head leaned back, his eyes wide under his furry brow. "Are you sure?"

Sabina didn't even glance at him when she nodded. Her thin lips pursed into a barely visible line and remained that way as the bearded man walked out of the greenhouse.

It was just me and her. The hair on the back of my neck rose as she eyed me up and down, her nostrils flaring. When her eyes shifted to the spot next to her, every single nerve in my body begged me to stay right here.

I swallowed and walked up to the bench, trembling as I sat next to her.

My upper arm brushed her shoulder and my teeth chattered.

She was as cold as the tundra, and even the air lacked oxygen.

I glanced over at her and again, an old corpse appeared in her place.

Then just as quickly, she was there, finally speaking, "I'm going to tell you a story. Do not speak until I am done."

I could only nod; she terrified me more than any shotgun.

Satisfied with my pitiful obedience, she took a low, hissing breath and began.

"A long, long time ago, there was a mighty King who ruled over a wealthy kingdom. A proud King, he believed that all he had laid eyes on, all he had stepped on, was his to rule.

Many smaller countries and tribes have tried to rebel against this King...and all have failed. His kingdom grew the more he conquered, growing fat from the blood of those who opposed him. No one could satiate his greed, and he was emboldened by countless victories. One might say that he had no good in him at all.

That was all the good inside of him went to his only child. A beautiful, happy babe who lifted the hearts of those who lined eyes on her. She was his prized possession and the only thing he loved.

On the babe's first birthday, the King held a celebration. A festival of wonder, where nobles would come and lay gifts and treasures in front of the royal cradle. Rulers from far-off lands would come with sages and lay magical blessings upon the child. Each gift and blessing was used to curry favor with the King, so that one of their princes would be betrothed to the princess.

Except for one.

For it was not a gift nor a blessing.

It was a curse.

A woman of magic, one you would call a witch, appeared before the cradle and cursed the babe within. A curse that would cost the cruel King all of his allies and toss the kingdom and all of its people into war after war until nothing of it was left."

Sabina paused, skeleton white fingers trembling before she tightly wound them together. I glanced at her hands and then at her face. She wore a sneer across her lips, but her brow knotted tightly together and the bottom lids of her eyes twitched.

"Sa-Sabina, you don't—"

She held up a finger, shaking her head, "I am not done."

I closed my mouth and looked at my own forearms, taking in the self-made cracks and divots in my skin.

She continued, her voice wavering.

"The curse was simple; the child would blossom into a beautiful woman. One she is of age, under the darkness of night, with only the light of the moon, she would entrance anyone who laid their eyes on her. She would be the fairest and most wonderful princess, the combination of all the blessings.

However, once the sun rose, she would turn into a horrific and vile thing. Those same people she entranced at night would only see her as their most hideous fears. Instead of the sun bringing warmth and love, all it would bring would be terror and hatred.

Of course, since she was a witch and the little infant was a princess, the only way to break the curse was just as simple.

A kiss.

A true love kiss in the sunlight, where the princess would be at her most hideous.

The King demanded that the witch take the curse away, but she could not. It was branded into the child's fate. The King imprisoned the foul witch, but that did him little good. The witch became a most willing audience, anticipating the havoc that would come."

She chuckled, but it was hollow; empty of joy.

"Of course, it would be years until the curse would take root. Many of the nobles had forgotten it altogether. Even the King, who aged with worry, grew content and complicit. The princess, growing more enchanting each day, would surely gain a kiss under the blessing of the sun.

The promised day had come and with it was another festival, celebrating not just the little princess's birth, but her coming of age. After that day, she would become a woman. The night was filled with jovial dancing and merry song; the princess had met her betrothed and her beauty won him over and the aged King looked up his dancing treasure with pride, seeing her glow in the moonlight...

But then the sun rose and the witch, deep in the dungeon, half-mad from starvation, surviving only by her hate, sang in triumph.

The festival erupted in horror, with the princess in the center.

Her betrothed took one look at her in the morning sun and flung himself off the palace balcony and onto a crowd of peasants. Guards, hardened by war, screeched in horror when they laid eyes upon her, many gauging out their eyes. The older ones simply collapsed onto the floor, their faces permanently carved in blinding fear. The sun had revealed their worst fears as a princess, now covered in blood and called a monster.

Her mother, a concubine, met the same fate as her betrothed, drowning herself in the fountain. The King was the only one who was hidden away from the sight of his own daughter, leaving her sobbing alone.

It didn't take long for the Kingdom to fall. The alliance was broken by the death of the prince. War ravaged the kingdom. The princess was hidden away, locked up in a gilded cage and the witch, now free as they all the guards had abandoned the cells, revelled in the destruction.

That awful Kingdom was in ruins, the King executed as a madman. The witch sang the songs of her dead people and danced among the corpses and flames.

Until she heard a wail.

A sorrowful wail from a girl who just became a woman, whose only crime was being born to the man the witch hated."

I blinked when she paused, stunned.

A glistening droplet fell down her chiseled cheeks. Then another, and another.

Her shoulders were trembling and though her jaw stayed set, tears kept pouring down her cheeks. Her knees were bouncing as her black eyes stared forward, taking in a memory.

Even though the story was...well bat-shit crazy, the intensity of her sadness and despair showed the truth in her words.

"Are you...you're a witch?"

Sabina nodded, her voice low and raspy, "I cursed that little girl to get back at the foul man who took away my home, my people, my...my daughters." She sniffed, making no motion to hide her cascading grief. "His soldiers raped, maimed, and murdered my people. They scorched my homeland. I only survived because of my magic, corrupted by hatred. Blinded by that hatred, I cursed a baby." Her eyes finally shifted downwards, towards her nails. It took me by surprise at how dirty her nails were. The tips were black with ash and dirt.

My heart pounded in my chest, the sound echoing in my ears, "If you're...The Witch. Then...Mallena..."

She nodded, "She is The Princess."

How the fuck?! "Kingdoms, long ago, that makes little sense! How is she still alive?!"

Sabina's black smudged fingers covered her mouth, "Because the curse is never-ending. Her life is bound to it, forever."

My eyes watered. I clenched my teeth and my fists, "Then...then you should break it! Why are you still punishing her? She did nothing wrong!"

"You think I don't know that?!" Her head twisted towards me and I can see the countless years in the deep crevices appearing on her face. "I spent centuries caring for that child! I have tried again and again to free her and I have FAILED every single time! The cure is just as simple as the curse, but not even I could do it!"

I balked, blinking back angry tears. "You're the one who sees her during the day! Don't you lo-love her like a daughter?!"

"Yes. I do..too much." Her head leaned up, staring at the stars, "I see my daughter every day. I see her with her neck bent, the bone protruding out of her skin. I see her cursing me for not saving her. Not saving her sisters. When the sun rises every morning, I see her and I forget what Mallena looks like. I failed my daughters and Mallena reminds me of that every time the sun shines on her face." She tilted her head and the void in her eye sockets glared at me. "I have to live with my failures and my fears every single day. What about you?"

The void in my head repeats.

Yeah, shit-bag, what about you?

Chapter Twenty-Two
The Broken Knight

I didn't know how to answer. This woman stared her fear and grief in the face every time the sun entered the manor and touched upon Mallena's skin.

Meanwhile, I screamed and crawled out at the sight of mine, pissing myself all the way.

Mallena, through no fault of her own, became my worst nightmare. Sabina had spent centuries with her. As unbelievable as this all was, she was right.

What about me?

"There has to be a way to help her." I whispered, helpless.

Sabina rolled her eyes, almost to the point where I coud only see the white, "Give it up. There is no way. If I can't bring myself to kiss the mutilated, wailing corpse of my eldest, then there is no hope for you." She lifted a thin, trembling hand, motioning past the glass windows and towards the tower, "You brought her hopes up and like everyone else, you let her down."

You let everyone down. You let Mr. Martinez down. Your therapist, your
brothers, your parents. No one can count on you. You just fail them.
You're a parasite that just wastes and waste until there is nothing left.

"She needs someone to try—"

"Shut up." Sabina lips curled upwards and the decrepit crone sat in her place, sneering at me with coal black eye sockets, "Shut up and leave. Leave Mallena at peace. You've done enough!"

That's not true.

I haven't done anything at all.

All Mallena wanted was to be happy and I didn't give that to her.

We stood together over the railing, staring at the street miles below. If I didn't push her back to the roof...

We would've dove together.

Splattering across the pavement.

She didn't join me to save me.

She just didn't want to die alone.

"Mallena can't have peace." My words are a raspy whisper, fighting against the cackling shouts of the fog drilled into the back of my brain. "She's left a lone when everyone else is asleep and the only person she sees during the day...hates her."

"I don't hate Mallena."

"She doesn't know that. All she knows is that you don't see her." I clench my fists, remembering Mallena screaming and sobbing. She didn't want me to look at her, but she wanted me to stay. "You don't really see her."

"Don't you dare claim to know her more than I do! You know nothing!"

She's right. I don't know jackshit.

But I know what it feels to lose hope. To not have friends. To watching the world move on without you. The sickness in my head, the void gobbling up all emotion and sensation until I am numb nothingness. I know that feeling.

I am sick, but I can...

Fuck this is so hard for me to say. The void keeps pushing it away but I have to say it. I have to.

"I can...I can ask for help. From my-my family. I can get help. But Mallena...what about her?"

Sabina's snarl shriveled away, her head leaning back, "There is no helping her."

My jaw is set and I turn my back, walking forward. Out of the greenhouse and towards the mansion.

That is not true.

There is a way.

I won't give up on her.

I won't let her be on the rooftop a lone, waiting for the void to tip her over.

I maybe a shitbag, but she deserves to live! That's the least I can do!

Icy claws reach out at my back, gripping my arms. I know Sabina is trying to stop me, to drag me away. The fog is screaming, choking my heart and weighing down my feet.

I keep walking.

"Cole! Don't you dare go in there! You leave her alone!"

That's all everyone has been doing! Everyone has been leaving her alone!

I hiss in agony as frozen nails tear at my wrist, tugging it free and shoving the double doors open. Once inside, I break into a sprint, using all the energy I can muster to climb the stairs. Going up further and further.

Until I see her door.

Her open door.

"Mallena?" I pause just before the threshold. It was...almost like the the last time we spent naked together. Just...off.

Something felt wrong about the room.

"Mallena?" The room didn't glow like it did that night; there was no hint of joy. The fairy lights were off, dust covered the food drawers and vanity. I gulped, stepping just inside the room to see torn clothes and dresses were strewn haphazardly along the floor. The glass french doors to the balcony were not just covered.

They were boarded up.

The silence was deafening.

I turned towards the footsteps coming closer, my eyes wide as I take in Sabina's glare. Her lips but I cut in first, "She's not here."

That dark gaze softens and her jaw grew slack as she pushed past me and entered the room. Her chin trembles, her composure gone, "I haven't seen her anywhere tonight. Except at dinner...she didn't eat."

"Where is she?"

She doesn't answer, turning away and jogging down the stairs.

Now I'm the one following her, looking down every hall before stepping to the foyer. I wasn't sure how it was possible but Sabina got even paler as she picked up her cell phone.

I knew she was calling Kenneth and when the chef ran out of the kitchen, she began to shout orders at him too. However, I did not stay to listen.

Mallena was missing.

I went back outside, sprinting to the greenhouse.

She wasn't there.

I went back towards the front courtyard, looking towards the gargoyles on the giant stone and iron gate. They glared back at me, accusing me.

She's missing because of you. She left because you came back.

She is cursed.

You're diseased.

They fed the void, letting it's ghostly voice echo in my brain. I shake my head, turning towards the woods. No fireflies danced among the leaves. No rainbow stars lit the treetops. They were just as dark and gloomy as they were during the day.

I swallowed, jogging along the edge of the woods. I'm sure Sabina was scouring the manor and chef must be frantically turning every single bush and planter towards the back gardens. I could hear Kenneth's truck roaring through the gate, his headlights beaming from behind me and lighting up the woods.

As well as a small dirt path.

I hissed as the cold night air dug into my scratches, my bottom lip trembling as I stared into those woods. The tree trunks bent and curved towards the path, black gnarled limbs guiding me deeper into the forest. I almost took a step forward, before my scratches stung again, the icy chill of a certain witch's stare gripping me back, "Let me go."

"Cole, I have one thing to ask you."

I glanced towards the sky, seeing the slightest glimmer of purple, "It's almost day. I need to find her."

"Why?! You weren't able to face her before!"

Goddammit, why must she always remind me! "I know! But I have to try again—" I shouted back at her, turning to glare at those blackhole eyes.

Only to see onyx gems staring at me, glistening. Sabina's face crumpled and she sniffed. In the greenhouse she had fought hard to remain stoic, even as tears froze on her cheeks. Now she couldn't. "Tell me. Even if it's just a lie." Kenneth put a hand on her shoulder, only for her to shove it off her gaunt shoulder, "Can you break the curse?!"

I have never seen a Santa Claus look so distraught and confused before. Honestly seeing Sabina look so lost, with glittering eyes and a upward furrowed brow made my stomach lurch.

She was counting on me.

You're going to fail. Like always. Just tell her the truth and bury your face into mud—

SHUT UP! JUST SHUT UP!

You know you can't do shit! You're just going to fail! Piss yourself again and curl up like a fucking maggot eating shit!

I don't care if I fail! I have to try!

So you're just going to lie? 'Fake it till you make it'?

I lifted my fist to the side my head, the knuckles pounding on it as I stared at the ground.

Sabina is counting on me.

Kenneth is staring at me, looking as helpless as I felt.

He is counting me.

Mallena...

She needs me.

I shove the void as deep down as I could, forcing my lips to move under the weight of the fog, "Yes. I can break it." I turn to the woods and without looking back, I take another step forward.

The icy claws let go of my skin. My feet feel heavy, weighed down by the fog.

I just keep walking forward.

To where Mallena has to be.

Chapter Twenty-Three
The Dawn's Kiss

Thank god I took the landscaping job, or else this would be hell.

I hissed as my knee slammed onto the pebble littered path. I wiped the sweat off my brow as I pushed myself up the narrow path before leaning against a tree trunk and gazing at the sky.

The deep blues of the night sky were blending in the purples and deep pinks of the coming morning. I didn't even know if she came up here—

"The view is amazing up here."

Where else would she go?

I took a shaky step forward, pulling myself further up while my thighs burned as the path wound left and up. "Mallena. Please be here."

I thought I heard a sigh traveling along the breeze. When I turned my head towards them, something rolled down towards me. A patter of shifting pebbles, rolling underneath, traveling with it. Considering the strangeness I have already witnessed, I wondered if the tiny little rocks and pieces of dirt were carrying the thing to me.

I recognized it.

It was a ballet flat, covered in thin layers of dirt, splattered with mud, but not torn or frayed. Little crystals lined edge; the fading moonlight caused tiny rainbows to shoot from each cut edge. I crawled upwards, taking it into my hand and holding it close.

I was no prince, and Mallena was no Cinderella.

Yet she was just as trapped, and this shoe was my proof that she was there.

Now I hiked upwards, one hand short and the path winding to a steep and narrow trail.

Sobs traveled downwind towards me, and I pivoted away from large rocks tumbling down. "Mallena?"

The sobs quieted to whimpers and then silence.

"Mallena, stop." I licked the salt from my upper lip, coarse stubble scratching my tongue. "Please stop."

A sniffle traveled down towards me, and I pushed myself up to meet it.

"I got your shoe." Those were the first words I gave to a suicidal ancient princess? Captain Obvious is all I got.

"Keep it." She responded, another sniffle following those words. She was moving again; the tumbling pebbles told me those.

"Mallena, please stop."

"You stop. You stop following me!" That command echoed uselessly in my ears.

I would not stop.

I would not run away this time.

I kept climbing after her and I don't think she cared anymore.

The pink sky crested towards the summit.

As I finally heaved myself upwards, to the top of the cliff, something else rolled past me, forcing a frown.

The other shoe dropped.

Please don't let me be too late.

I pulled myself onto the edge, sucking in air that I desperately needed. My heart raced a thousand miles per hour as I glanced around the top. "Ma-Mallena-"

"Cole, why did you come back?"

I jerked my head towards her voice, and my neck popped. My heart finally took a break seeing her, leaning over a two-bar railing and towards the horizon, "I-I had to."

She sniffed again, her shoulders hunched as I limped closer. "Don't Cole. Please don't come closer."

"Mallena, I'm sorry." I stood next to her.

There was no trace of the roasted abomination from that day; only dirty surrounded me, not melting, rotted flesh. On the edge of that cliff, all I heard were her muted sobs, not the choir of screams.

Yet my heart still shattered, and my stomach sank into an acidic pit.

Those night-sky eyes were devoid of sparkling stars, and her pink-tinted cheeks were marred by dirt and tears. Her posture stiffened as I came close and her lips trembled while pressed tightly together. "It's not your fault. You didn't know."

"I should've left when you asked me." If only I punched myself instead, but the void glared at me with enough loathing. "I just wanted to be close to you. When you left that first night...I didn't want that to happen again and that was fucking shitty of me." I swallowed heavily, watching her grip the railing. "I'm sorry."

Her lips twitched up with eyes as empty as hers. There was no smile. "You know, I wanted that too. I should have kicked you out, but I thought that...maybe this would be different. You would be different." She clenched her teeth and held up her hands, "Not like you not being you, because...I wanted to wake up next to you and watch your face light up in the sun." Her fingers closed into her palm. "I wanted you to wake up against my chest and kiss me, over and over, before saying 'good morning'. I wanted that so-so much!"

I looked at her trembling fist and, beyond my control, my fingers reached out towards it, so close to stroking the back of her hand.

Only for her to pull away and finally turn towards me. It was as if a dam broke, and she wailed, "But that didn't happen! You didn't see me!" Her fingers stretched out and covered her face. She hacked out sobs, "Even I reached out, you screamed and crawled away from me!"

"Mallena, I know that's what happened, and I wished I could take it back and be-be brave—"

"But you can't!" I tried to reach for her again, and she pulled away. "No one can! I am a monster! I have been a monster for so long! The sun mocks me while I hide, praying I don't cause someone to commit suicide! I force myself to smile every night so no one would worry, but I am rotting inside!" Her arms curled around herself and in seeing her face, centuries of agony flowed out with every word, "I am ROT, Cole. I am rotting and filth and no matter how hard I try for people to look at me, to believe in me, to love me...The sun reveals how disgusting I am."

"Mallena, you are not disgusting! I will never think of you like that! I love you!" Please, believe me, Mallena.

Her brow knotted downward, and she whimpered with the shake of her head. "No, Cole. That's...that's not enough anymore." She looks forward and I follow her gaze.

The horizon is turning pink with a thin line of yellow.

The night was retreating and the sun that Mallena feared so much was rising over the edge.

A creak from metal against stone made me jerk my head back, and I lunged forward as Mallena climbed to the other side of the railing. My other hand released the flat, letting fall onto the shimmering lake as I wrapped my arms around her, holding her away from that perilous edge with my embrace. "Stay right here! Please..."

"I can't, Cole...I can't do that anymore."

She is trying so hard to pull away from me and dive into the abyss.

The same abyss I wanted for so long, yet she pulled me from it.

"Mallena, we can look at more views. Have more late night talks. Do whatever you want. You have so much to offer, so much more than me." I shuddered, my forehead pressed against the back of her head. I could pull her back, kicking and screaming from the edge if I had to.

But I didn't want her to scream and be locked up in a big house alone.

I didn't want her to stay trapped in the same shitty life she lived, watching the world move without her.

I wanted her happy.

"That's not enough. Please let me go!" The yellow rays reaching up from the skyline and she was twisted against me, struggling to push me away. "I don't want you to see me like that again! I can't have you screaming because of me!" Her hands gripped my forearms, but instead of pulling them away, she held them against her chest, "I can't have you run away again..."

I know that if I let her go...then I would never see her again.

She would run away, and I wouldn't be able to catch her.

I would rather DIE than let that happen.

More than any void in my head and more than the fog dragging my brain down into the mud and shit of my existence, I would rather jump with her.

She deserves to be happy.

We deserve to be happy.

"Mallena, I won't run away again. We'll face this together." I watched sun reaching across the lake as the purple left the sky and then I pulled back, only to climb over the railing and hold her again, pressing her head against my chest. "I want to see the sun with you. If the night is not enough, then I will face the day with you. I promise."

"Cole...please don't look at me." Her fingers gripped my back, clawing into my shirt, her voice dissolving into gargling whimpers as the sun cascaded over us.

I closed my eyes tightly as smoke filled the air and harsh gales of sand replaced rustling leaves, cutting into my skin. There was no moisture in the air; my lips split open and blood coated my tongue.

It wasn't real.

This wasn't real.

Yet no matter how many times I screamed that in my head, I couldn't open my eyes. The winds carried sand that cut open old scars and screams roared through the crackling inferno that was once the lake. My forearms sunk into Mallena's body; her skin was melting from her muscles and bones and the molten gore seared my flesh.

It felt real.

The erupting screams and crackling of fire sounded real.

Sulfur, ash, and roasting flesh flew into my nostrils and tasted real.

My knees were about to buckle and if I didn't lean against the railing, I would plummet down into Hell.

All of my memories and my fears were in my arms, and I wanted to puke.

Tears forced my eyelids open. Stinging tears that mixed into open wounds, I could feel the shrapnel dig and tear into my skin as my brothers screamed in agony, desperate to pull their limbs back together as their screams and curses joined the ones in Arabic.

Why did I live?

Why didn't I die?

Why does it keep hurting this much?

When I looked down and instead of starry eyes, there were black holes with jelly streaming down dissolving cheeks. A face contorted in a piercing choir of hatred and pain as pus burst from the many boils on this cooking, burning body that writhed and quaked in agony.

My hands let go of its body only to hold those gore dripping cheeks in my palms, watching my fingers char with skin turning black, then flaking away to expose bone and muscle.

Sabina faced her fears every day, and I did too.

The ravenous void digging into my brain, was the fear and guilt that sucked away energy and hope. I thought Mallena could chase that away while I kept running from it.

I couldn't run anymore and Mallena carried so much sorrow by herself.

I can't force someone else to take it.

My lips parted to scream before I clenched them close.

I can't run from it, so I will accept it.

She deserves to be happy and so do I.

"Mallena..." I pulled the screaming, fleshless skull closer, a smile on my face as I witness every single horror all over again, "I love you."

As the world erupted into flames, my lips pressed against hers.

Hell was never sweet as this; even if I die of a heart attack, this was worth it.

Chapter Twenty-Four
Sunrise

I didn't know what to expect.

I wasn't sure if it would be a beam of light or a glittery explosion. With my eyes closed and my lips pressed against the scream, melting face of the woman I loved, I was in no place to observe what was happening.

I just wanted to keep holding her, leaning against the railing. It was only when I felt small fingers against my chest did I finally pull back.

I was still scared shitless, though. My eyes stayed closed even though I no longer smelled burning corpses. My shoulders trembled as I braced myself for the day.

"Cole..."

My name in her voice sounded sweeter than any song and, yes, that was cheesy and I don't give a fuck.

"Cole, open your eyes."

My eyes opened only a millimeter, and I winced, shutting them as blinding, burning light stung them.

"Cole, I need you to look at me."

I gulped, nodding before I opened my eyes, squinting at the morning light.

Light blue skies with a hint of peach and yellow.

The lake shimmering with glittering rays of sun.

I looked behind me, seeing mountain crevices and trees.

Then finally, I looked forward and down, my hands gripping her hips, fingers trembling, "Ma-Mallena..."

Mallena, with starry night eyes glistening like galaxies, grinned through crystal tears. "Do you see me?"

I choked on my answer, my own cheeks stained with hot tears. Fuck, I was crying again, but I was so fucking happy.

I lifted her up and kissed her again. Her arms wrapped around my neck, leaning against me as she kissed me back, sobbing into my mouth.

I saw her.

In the full morning sun, under blue skies with singing birds.

When we finally pulled apart, desperate for air, she released a gasping laugh, a flush across her cheeks, "Cole! I'm free...! We're free!"

I couldn't help but laugh too, looking up at her and finally feel...relief.

Complete, calming relief.

I may not have a lot of fairytales...

But I have seen a few movies.

Just as my heart stopped sprinting 100 miles per hour, the rock under my feet shook,

Then loosened.

We were on a cliff overlooking the lake on the estate.

Now...we were falling.

I couldn't turn fast enough and the railing bent with the stone.

I tried to grab it with one hand, keeping the other tightly around Mallena...only for my fingers to graze the metal.

Just as we smiled together. Just when the world seemed right again...we were falling together.

I would cackle at the bullshit of it all if I wasn't embracing the woman I wanted to save.

I thought I saved her.

Instead, I damned her.

I damned us.

How fucking ironic.

Time slowed down when you're about to die.

I could take it from the rocks falling beside us. The edge of the cliff fading further and further away while the glittering water was coming closer and closer.

I braced myself, trying to get my body as straight as I could. I wasn't an Olympic diver, and I was holding a woman who closed her eyes, pursing her lips as she silently accepted our unfair fate.

We were going to die.

Just when we finally wanted to move on.

We were falling so slowly towards the water that will rip us apart.

The water that was rising to meet us.

While my fingers tied themselves into her hair, I also closed my eyes.

Did we die on impact?

I felt the icy fluid rush against our skin, but no pain or shock.

My teeth shattered, and goosebumps grew all over my skin, so I know I was still alive. When I opened my eyes, Mallena shivered against me, her black hair matted against her face. I stared into her eyes as we both realized that somehow...we survived.

"How...how the fuck?!" Those were the only words that came to mind and yes, I sounded incredibly stupid.

Mallena looked away from me, gripping my upper arms before as she looked all around us. "We're floating! How are we floating?!"

She was right.

We were floating on a wave formed from the lake. A wave guiding us towards the shore. I turned my head towards that shoreline.

I know that after all I have been through, nothing should surprise me anymore.

However, when I think back on my experiences before this moment, I remembered reflecting that there was some kind of explanation. I was so fucked in the head anything could be a hallucination.

That Sabina, Mallena, everyone was fucking with me somehow.

Yet I can't explain this.

I can't explain watching the platinum straw haired woman holding up her arms and using her hands to guide the water, bringing us to safety. I couldn't explain, as we got closer, her age shifting between her thirties and then her centuries.

Sabina didn't believe in miracles and neither did I.

Sabina was a witch.

In every sense of the word.

While I was dumbstruck, Mallena began screaming towards her warden, "NO! Stop it! Sabina, stop it! Let us down! Please stop!" No longer was she fearing for her life.

The panic in her voice was for Sabina, whose knees buckled, but her arms stayed up.

Only when Kenneth ran from his parked truck, only when we were pulled onto shore, did the witch lowered her arms.

She collapsed.

I shuddered and limped with Mallena. We were holding each other up as we got closer to the coughing woman.

"Sabina!" Kenneth made it to Sabina first, kneeling beside her as she vomited up black soot and bile. Her body kept shifting between forms, growing thinner and gaunt. Finally, with one last gasp, the shifting stopped.

Before us was an ancient woman, whose eyes, sunken into her skull, were a clear grey.

"Why...why did you save us?" Mallena pulled away from me, her fingers tracing mine before she knelt down. "Why did you do that?"

The rasping crone's lips pulled upward into a smile. It was gentle and warm. In this moment, she looked more human than ever. "I took away centuries of your life. Your happiness." Wrinkled fingers reached up towards Mallena's face. Despite the emptiness in her eyes, I wondered if this was the first time she looked at the princess. "Now that you're free...I couldn't let it go to waste."

"But you're going to die. Look at you! You're dying!"

A chuckle left the old woman's dry lips, and she had remnants of Sabina's smirk. "About time." Her hand stroked Mallena's cheek, then fell against her shoulder. "It's about time I go to my daughters and their children."

"Sabina, we can...I have my truck, I can go get help." Kenneth, the muscular Santa Claus he was, sounded helpless. We both were dumbstruck bystanders, peeking at a moment between a guardian and her child.

His words were empty, and the witch knew it, dismissing them with the slightest shake of her head. "I need to go home." A breath left her lips, and those eyes were now on me. There was no hatred, no cold anger and loathing.

She reminded me of my grandmother, giving me a kiss on the forehead before leaving the world forever.

That smile stayed on her lips, even as her body crumbled like sand, "Thank you...for letting me see the princess...one more time..." Her eyes closed and her smile widened, "Live and don't screw up this time, Cole..."

I sat down beside Mallena as she released agonized sobs, trying to grasp onto the white crystals remains of her only friend. Kenneth lowered down, resting his elbows on his knees, his lips pursed under his beard as he wiped his eyes.

I silently held my exhausted and crying princess, thinking of the last words Sabina said.

...She was a witch to the end.

I won't screw up.

I have a life to live.

Chapter Twenty-Five
Happily Ever After

My stomach twisted and turned as the medication hit it. It was far more bearable now than before, but I still didn't like it. I leaned back against the passenger side door as my stomach lurched back to normal with my slow breaths. My eyes shifted to my phone as I typed out an update in a group text.

It was a little embarrassing, but my therapist recommended it, so enough people were on my ass about the meds.

The group only comprised my parents and Mr. Martinez, but it was the right amount of humiliation to keep me honest without trashing my phone out of frustration.

When I came back home, my parents were relieved and angry. Honestly, I rather they yelled at me; instead, their mild scolding came with a hug.

The void almost cheered with the disappointment.

It's still there, hanging around in the back of my head. It'll always be there, but at least I'm dealing with it the best I can.

The crew arrived at the estate, only to see Kenneth escort Mallena to his truck.

They had questions, but Mr. Martinez saw my face and figured I saw enough shit.

I wish I could've told him I wouldn't break down...but I shouldn't make promises I couldn't keep.

From what he told me, he got a story from Kenneth a few days later. That Sabina fell ill, quietly passed away. Mr. Martinez wanted to go to the funeral, pay his respects, but there would not be one. Sabina didn't have any family.

Only Mallena.

Mallena who cried into the crystal remains of her surrogate fairy god witch-mother.

So instead of a funeral, Kenneth continued the contract and we (I got my job back...another reason I have the group text) would go back and get the grounds ready for donation. I guess it's gonna be a 'historic' property or something.

Mallena didn't live there anymore.

"I can't stay here anymore. Not by myself. I need to get away, you know?"

I know.

So Ken has been running the place until becomes part of history and its grounds considered a National Forest. Fitting, I guess.

I set the phone in my pocket, leaning my head back. The deep oranges and purples of the sky brought a cool breeze that felt good on my skin. Even along with my scars. They didn't itch as much, though some days are...

Not gonna lie.

Some days fucking suck.

There it was, that fog in the back of my head, weakly clawing.

The void was my constant companion.

My head turned at the sound of familiar footsteps, my lips up in a smile, "Hey babe."

Mallena giggled, shifting her hat shyly. "Sorry I made you wait. It's weird...walking with the sun out."

I stood up straighter, holding out my arms. She walked closer, then fell forward against my chest. I closed my arms around her, my cheek against her hat, "Are you okay? We can postpone dinner."

She was still for a moment, before I felt her head shift from side to side. "I made your parents wait long enough. I want to meet them."

I tilted my head, one hand moving under her chin so I give a plant a kiss on her cheek, "You might regret that."

Another giggle and she glanced up at me with a raised eyebrow, eyes sparkling like galaxies. "I'm with you. They can't be all bad."

I tried not to laugh as I opened the door for her. I glanced down at a clear pendant dandling from the chain draped around her neck. Crystal shards glittered against her golden, tanned skin.

I'm doing my best, Sabina.

As I entered the car, my girlfriend was next to me. I let out a shuddering breath. We were both broken in our own ways...but we're going through this together.

Hopefully stronger for it.

I pulled away from her apartment, my free hand resting on the middle console. Mallena's fingers gently stroked my palm, before intertwining with my fingers. With a soft squeeze, I drove forward to my parents' house.

Towards the setting sun.

Coming Soon!

C ould the love between a Sinner and a Saint only end in flames?

Birth of a Sin Vol. 1 is coming soon to a Online Storefront near you!

Enjoyed This Book?
Check Out These Titles Next!

Drained: A Vampire Noir

Genre: Gothic Mystery Horror
Storefront: Free To Read[1]

The Story of Red and Her Wolf

Genre: Dark Fairytale Fantasy
Storefront: Free To Read[2]

1.   https://storyoriginapp.com/giveaways/ff94d52a-3660-11ec-8c33-8b12ffea6aa5

2.   https://storyoriginapp.com/giveaways/bcf34516-3107-11ec-8858-0326fab3efe4

Want the Latest on Coda Languez and Her Other Works?

S ign up for her Newsletter![1]
    Fill Your Inbox with Funny Anecdotes, WebSerial and Novel Updates, Bodacious Art, Special Promos and adorable Corgi Pictures!

---

1. https://codemonkeyarts.com/newsletter/

Don't miss out!

Visit the website below and you can sign up to receive emails whenever Coda Languez publishes a new book. There's no charge and no obligation.

https://books2read.com/r/B-A-NDAT-VGGXB

BOOKS 2 READ

Connecting independent readers to independent writers.

Also by Coda Languez

The Curse of Dawn

Watch for more at https://codemonkeyarts.com.

About the Author

Coda Languez is a Software Engineer by day and an Artist/Author by night. She is lover of all things anime, horror, and comic related, making her a true geek in all aspects. Heavily influenced by the works of Satoshi Kon, Kouta Hirano, Francesca Lia Block, and Clive Barker, Coda mixes black comedy, horror, magic realism, and dark romance into her works, creating an 'it's complicated' relationship between readers and her anti-heroic, even villainous protagonists.

When she is not programming in her day job or writing psychological terrifying romances and dark action comedies in the night hours, Coda often binges on anime, fantasy, and sci-fi sagas and indulges in competition reality tv (a guilty pleasure). She is the mother of an adorable toddler and his Pembroke Welsh Corgi brothers, and wife to an awesome and often exasperated husband.

For information on Coda's latest works, connect with her on social media via @codemonkeyarts.

Read more at https://codemonkeyarts.com.

CPSIA information can be obtained
at www.ICGtesting.com
Printed in the USA
BVHW041111090522
636524BV00030B/1429